'So, he is yo

Dori said, anger   her eyes.

Sal sat on the ed   certain what she was talking about. However, he had heard that tone before and it put him on the defensive.

'What do you mean?'

She sank into the chair Diego had just vacated. She looked tired as well as irritated. 'I mean that he just reached for you as though he knows you.'

'Knows me,' he repeated, waiting for the words to make sense. 'How could he know me? You just walked in with him.'

She appeared off balance, uncertain. 'He looks just like you,' she said.

He looked into the baby's face, wondering what on earth Dori was trying to say. 'He could be a Dominguez,' he said, as the baby tried to remove his tie through his neck. 'But if you recall,' he said, peeling back little fingers to free himself, 'I haven't been anywhere near you in two years.'

'Well, what does that have to do with anything?' she demanded, coming to help disengage the little fingers. *I'm* not his mother.'

Dear Reader,

Welcome to the wonderful world of Special Edition!

This month we're continuing Muriel Jensen's immensely popular WHO'S THE DADDY? series with *Daddy in Demand* which we've chosen as our THAT'S MY BABY! story.

Renowned author Laurie Paige gives us the second intense instalment of the WINDRAVEN LEGACY with *When I See Your Face*. While Gina Wilkins kicks off her brand-new HOT OFF THE PRESS trilogy with *The Stranger in Room 205*—an amnesia tale with a striking twist.

Meanwhile, Christine Scott brings us *Storming Whitehorn* which is the last of the four MONTANA BRIDES books. Plus, a modern fairytale comes from Barbara McMahon in *Starting with a Kiss*, and then there's a rugged loner wondering if he's husband and father material in *Stranger in a Small Town* by Ann Roth.

Enjoy!

The Editors

Daddy in Demand
MURIEL JENSEN

DID YOU PURCHASE THIS BOOK WITHOUT A COVER?
If you did, you should be aware it is **stolen property** as it was reported *unsold and destroyed* by a retailer. Neither the author nor the publisher has received any payment for this book.

All the characters in this book have no existence outside the imagination of the author, and have no relation whatsoever to anyone bearing the same name or names. They are not even distantly inspired by any individual known or unknown to the author, and all the incidents are pure invention.

All Rights Reserved including the right of reproduction in whole or in part in any form. This edition is published by arrangement with Harlequin Enterprises II B.V. The text of this publication or any part thereof may not be reproduced or transmitted in any form or by any means, electronic or mechanical, including photocopying, recording, storage in an information retrieval system, or otherwise, without the written permission of the publisher.

This book is sold subject to the condition that it shall not, by way of trade or otherwise, be lent, resold, hired out or otherwise circulated without the prior consent of the publisher in any form of binding or cover other than that in which it is published and without a similar condition including this condition being imposed on the subsequent purchaser.

Silhouette, Silhouette Special Edition and Colophon are registered trademarks of Harlequin Books S.A., used under licence.

*First published in Great Britain 2002
Silhouette Books, Eton House, 18-24 Paradise Road,
Richmond, Surrey TW9 1SR*

© Muriel Jensen 2001

ISBN 0 373 04889 0

23-0702

*Printed and bound in Spain
by Litografia Rosés S.A., Barcelona*

To Cathleen Riley—
high-school buddy, long-term friend.

MURIEL JENSEN

Muriel Jensen always wanted to be a writer. She grew up in southeastern Massachusetts but her family moved to Los Angeles when she was 10. Before becoming a writer Muriel worked for Pacific Telephone, the secretarial pool for the *Los Angeles Times* and has managed a bookstore.

Today, she has three adult children, a growing army of grandchildren, four cats and a Labrador retriever–mix named Amber. Muriel and her husband live in an old Victorian home on a hill overlooking the Columbia River. Every day Muriel watches sea-vessels come and go and speculates about the relationships of those aboard, and those they've left behind. She says it always inspires her.

SILHOUETTE SPECIAL EDITION

proudly continues
Muriel Jensen's *extremely popular mini-series*

WHO'S THE DADDY?

with

DADDY IN DEMAND
(also a That's My Baby! story)
July 2002

and

DADDY TO BE DETERMINED
August 2002

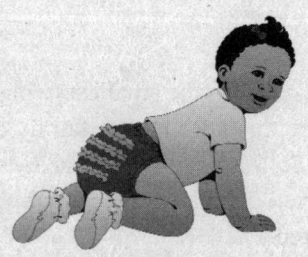

PROLOGUE

DORI MCKEON STIRRED restlessly among the tangled sheets as the familiar scene played itself out in her recurring dream.

There was a small adobe church in a dusty little square in the Mezquital Valley in the state of Hidalgo, Mexico. Music rose from an old pipe organ, and the carved pews were filled with people dressed in bright colors, singing. In the front of the church was an ornate gold altar that had been brought from Spain in the seventeenth century intended for a church in San Antonio and "diverted" by enterprising bandits when the ship ran aground.

A couple stood at the altar exchanging vows—a small dark-haired young woman in a white cotton dress and the traditional mantilla, and a tall, smiling man in a dark suit. In deference to the bride, the service was being conducted in English.

She was the bride.

Dori could feel her joy, and just the smallest twinge of guilt that she was doing this without her family in attendance. But she and Sal had been apart so long, and he wanted to be married quickly, before anything could interfere. She'd agreed.

"Do you, Salvatore Mateo Dominguez, take this woman, Dorianne Margaret McKeon..."

The vows continued; they promised to love each other forever, as the scent of jacarandas wafted through the open windows.

She'd never been this happy, this sure of who she was in her entire life. She was a daughter, a sister, a teacher. She was the woman who loved Sal Dominguez—the woman *he* loved.

Then the carved double doors of the church burst open with a loud bang and four men hurried into the church.

"No," Dori said aloud. "Not this ending. I want the one where we leave the church and fly home to Oregon and build a house in Dancer's Beach! The one where we have six children!"

But her subconscious was intent on replaying the end of her wedding the way it had happened. She watched with a helpless sense of loss.

She recognized the two younger men as Miguel and Eduardo, Julie's brothers.

"It's Desideria," one of them said. "Paco's out of jail. There was an auto accident during a prisoner transfer, and he escaped. We came for you right away."

Sal said something in Spanish that brought a gasp from the wedding guests.

Dori always saw this part in slow motion.

Sal turned to her, his handsome features set in hard lines, love for her visible under the anger in his eyes. "I have to go," he said simply.

She'd stammered. "Wh-What do you mean? We're getting married!"

He kissed one of her hands. "We *are* married. I am yours and you are mine. You will wait here, and Diego and Manuela will take care of you until I return."

Diego was his right-hand man in the company he'd formed to build the hospital. Manuela was Diego's wife.

"I'm married to you, not to them," she'd said firmly. "I came all this way—"

He squeezed her hand and interrupted. "I know, *chica,* but this is important. A life-and-death matter. You must understand."

"I don't," she'd insisted stubbornly.

She'd met Desideria Cabral, a tall, slender woman with elegant features who'd been volunteering her decorating skills and consulting with Sal several times a day. The woman had smiled at him every time he passed her as he walked over the site. And on occasion, Dori had seen her touch his arm or his hand.

Dori had been grateful when Desideria had left for home several days before the wedding. She'd even wondered if it would have been too hard for the woman to watch Sal marry someone else.

"Then you will wait here until I return," he said with a charming smile, "and can explain it to you."

"Why—?" she'd begun, but one of the two older men with Julie's brothers had interrupted.

"Salvatore! There is not much time."

Sal had framed her face in his hands and kissed

her. She'd been too astonished by the turn of events to stop him.

Then, with a last look at her, his hand touching hers, he backed away until his fingertips were out of reach. He turned and ran with his friends out of the church. She heard the sound of horses galloping away.

Her own screech of anger woke her.

Dori sat up in the frail light of a June morning and blinked at the tiny dimensions of her blue-and-white bedroom in suburban Edenfield. She groaned and fell back against her pillows with relief—or disappointment. She wasn't sure.

Well. You couldn't expect happy endings when you married a thief.

She and Sal had a tempestuous history filled with strong attraction and intermittent hostility. His self-imposed role as her protector had embarrassed and annoyed her, and her resistance to his protection had surprised and angered him.

Their situation had been dangerous, unusual, and not at all conducive to romance.

Dori's friend, Julie Godinez, had been part of the same family of thieves that Sal had also belonged to. Dori and Julie had gone to college together, and Julie had explained that her father, her uncle, her brothers, and her cousin, as well as several friends, had banded together to form the Cat Pack. They stole jewelry from the wealthy, converted it to cash, then returned with it to Madre Maria to support the impoverished village.

Julie, who had also been part of the Pack, had eventually quit to pursue her education. Her father had been furious and they'd had a terrible row. One day Dori had found Julie sobbing over a newspaper headline that read, "Cat Pack foiled but leader at Large." The subhead said, "Godinez's daughter sought for questioning."

Julie suspected that the gang had been set up, and she feared that her father would think she'd done it because of their argument. She was going into hiding so that she couldn't be taken in for questioning about her father, but she wanted to contact him to tell him she had not betrayed him.

Dori had had a plan. "My brother Duncan's going to Mexico to do a film," she'd said. "And they need a translator to work with the extras. Is that perfect?"

Julie had hugged her. "Yes. If you can put me in touch with the right person, I'll be forever grateful. But, Dori, I need you to do one more thing."

That was the point at which she should have walked away, Dori realized now. But Julie was her friend. She'd wanted Dori to contact her cousin, Salvatore Dominguez, who was in hiding with her father in a place known only to the family and make it clear that she had not been the one who'd betrayed them.

While Julie was in Mexico with the film crew, Dori had been dealing with Salvatore Dominguez. He'd been autocratic and overbearing from the beginning, refusing to let her see Julie's father, who'd been injured escaping the police after an attempt to rob the penthouse of a New Orleans hotel.

Their haphazard communication had gone on for ten months, during which time she'd tried hard to focus also on her thesis on novelists of the nineteenth century for her master's degree in English Literature.

She'd been returning from Nova Scotia, where she'd been researching with the foremost expert on Jane Austen, and was supposed to take in a theater performance in New York, when Sal intercepted her at the airport.

She'd barely had a moment to express surprise that he was there before he told her someone would claim her luggage later and pushed her ahead of him into a cab. There was about to be a confrontation, he told her, between Julie's father and Suarez, the man they were convinced had betrayed him to the police. Sal thought it best to keep her out of everyone's reach until it was over. He had a plan, he said, to make it all end happily.

He'd hidden her in an elegant suite at the Plaza. She remembered plush white-and-gold rooms, and being worried about her family who might be worried about *her,* and being afraid for Julie. She'd shouted at Sal, flung accusations, vented her frustrations, and finally dissolved into tears—something she never did.

He'd caught her hand and pulled her into his arms. And that was when everything had changed. At least for her.

She still couldn't remember who kissed whom, but it had been a revelation. She'd stared at him in amazement, and he'd looked at her with a new possessive attitude.

Then there'd been the phone call, the sudden flight to Sandy Gables, Florida, and all the unreal events of the next few days.

When they'd finally returned to Dancer's Beach with Duncan and Julie and her family, Sal had proposed marriage.

Dori had declined and they'd argued. He'd finally left for Mexico with a healthy contribution from her brother to enlarge Madre Maria's small hospital and add a children's wing, which the area needed desperately.

Her loneliness had been painful and had made every day seem interminable, even though she had earned her master's degree and had gotten a job teaching English at the local high school.

And then one day in late June she had caught a plane to Mexico City, and hired a private plane to Madre Maria. The pilot, who kept a beat-up old truck at the airport, drove her to the hospital.

The building had two stories and was modern in construction, except for several arches in the front and a bell tower. Inside was chaos. Wires dangled and plumbing stood up awkwardly where walls had been framed but remained unfinished.

Sal walked out of a side corridor, distracted by the contents of a sheaf of papers in his hand, and walked into her.

He'd grasped her arms with a smile of apology. "I'm so sorry, I..." And then he'd recognized her.

The moment had been electric. Possibly even nuclear.

They'd flown into each other's arms.

She'd agreed to be his wife.

She could remember now how she'd felt, standing at the altar, looking into his eyes. She'd never been that happy, that sure of who she was in her entire life. She was the woman who loved Sal Dominguez, the woman *he* loved.

"For all the good it's done me," she told herself now as she sat up again.

Two years of the wedding dream was enough! she decided. It was time to change things, to change herself. She couldn't alter the past. But she could darn well redirect her future—which at this point was going nowhere.

She liked teaching, but she'd always planned to write a book about the women of Georgian England. The events of her wedding day had taken their toll on her self-esteem and her trust in her ability to make sound decisions. So she'd stayed with teaching because it was safer than risking rejection from agents and publishers.

She threw the covers aside, climbed out of bed and went to the window. Edenfield, Oregon, stretched out before her, rooftops and chimneys and the tops of ash trees, cedars and Douglas firs.

She felt a longing for the coast and the peace she always found there—particularly when her family was somewhere else. Right now, she remembered as she warmed to the idea, her brothers and their wives and children were touring Europe for a month. Her father had just had knee replacement surgery, so he and her mother would be unable to follow her if she went to her brothers' summer house in Dancer's Beach.

That was it. The perfect place to turn her life in a new direction. She'd take her laptop, start her book, query several agents with the outline she'd prepared two years ago.

Then she'd hire a lawyer and get a divorce.

Pleased with her decision, she went into the kitchen to put on the kettle. As she filled it under the cold water faucet, she glanced at the calendar hanging on the side of the cupboard. Duncan and Julie had given it to her. Every month featured a different photo of their then two-year-old daughters.

This was Tuesday, June 26.

She gasped. How appropriate that she'd awakened with determination on this of all days.

She'd been married two years ago today.

CHAPTER ONE

"CONTAINS ISOFLAVONES." Dori read the nutrition panel on the back of the bag of toasted soy nuts. She couldn't remember what those were, but recalled that they had fat-fighting properties, and that they were a must for menopausal women. She dropped them into her cart.

At 26, she was far from that stage of her life, but fighting fat was something she should begin to consider, particularly if her book continued to go as well as it had been for the past three weeks. She'd done little but work and sleep, except for taking an occasional walk on the beach and a trip to town for groceries.

Last week, she'd run into Gusty and Bram Bishop, but had turned down their invitation to dinner, explaining that she was on a creative roll and was reluctant to distract herself in any way and risk a slowdown. Fortunately, they'd understood.

She phoned her parents every few days and was forced to endure the predictable lecture that a woman needed a healthy body as well as a healthy mind, and that she wouldn't be able to maintain either if she didn't get out into the fresh air and meet people.

By meeting "people," Dori knew, they meant "meeting men."

Her parents and her brothers had no idea she was married. In her family of charismatic, overachieving siblings, she'd always felt left out because of her gender, her inclination to be more academic than charming, and her place as the youngest child.

Her parents still thought of her as "the baby." She was sure it wouldn't matter how old she became, she would always be the baby. When she refused her mother's advice, the same guidance always came back to her in a chat with one of her brothers, or, since they'd married, one of her sisters-in-law.

She hadn't wanted to prove to any of them that they'd been right in their concerns about her ability to take care of herself. Or to let them even suspect that she was crushed by her mistake and didn't trust herself, either.

Though her mother had mentioned on more than one occasion that Sal had visited them, she'd never mentioned the marriage, and Dori had to believe he'd kept the secret also. If he had not, her mother would have interrogated her about it and reminded her that Dori had been warned against just such an error in judgment. Her entire family had liked Sal and would probably take his side, proving to her once again that she was the root of most of her own problems.

So, she'd been married for two years and no one north of the Mexican border knew, except the groom. According to her mother's report after Sal's last visit, he owned and operated a security company in Seattle. She'd provided Dori with the address.

That was good, she thought with brittle sarcasm as she snatched a bag of blue corn chips off the shelf. Then he could run to the aid of every beautiful woman who crossed his path, and even get paid for it—

"Dori!"

A cart collided with Dori's as she turned down the freezer aisle, studying a can of bean-and-cheese dip.

"Gusty!" she exclaimed. "Hi!"

The pretty redhead in a flower-sprigged sundress laughed. "No, I'm Athena."

Dori frowned apologetically. "I'm sorry, I'll never learn to tell the three of you apart." Gusty and her sisters were identical triplets who'd moved to Dancer's Beach the year before. The circumstances had been mysterious, but now the sisters were an important part of the community. Dori had met Gusty's sisters at Gusty's wedding nine months earlier.

"You're the lawyer?" Dori asked.

"That's right. I have an office in the Bijou Theater building."

"I was just thinking about making an appointment to see you."

Athena delved into the large purse in the baby carrier part of the cart and handed her a business card. "Please do. I can handle most things."

Dori lowered her voice. "Annulment? Divorce?"

Athena blinked and leaned across her cart. "I didn't think you were married," she said quietly.

There! She'd taken a giant step forward! "It's a long story. We were married and separated the same day. My family doesn't even know. The wedding took place in Mexico."

Athena had the grace to appear unaffected by what she'd heard. "In a civil ceremony?"

"No. In the Catholic Church."

Athena hesitated a moment, then nodded. "Well, come and see me, and we'll get on it."

"Thank you. When will David's book be out?"

She smiled broadly and patted a slightly paunchy stomach. "We'll both have a new edition out in November."

Dori offered her congratulations. "That's exciting. Do you know if it's a boy or a girl?"

"It's a girl," she replied, clearly delighted. "We're raising David's two younger brothers, you know, so we're all thrilled, the boys included."

They parted, with Dori promising to call Athena's office for an appointment.

Focusing on her groceries again, Dori inspected the fat content of the bean-and-cheese dip and retraced her steps to put it back. She examined the contents of her cart: sardines, a can of chili, several frozen dinners, a package of cranberry-nut English muffins, a box of English Breakfast tea, cheese, crackers, salsa, and the chips and soy nuts.

She'd almost forgotten chocolate. She picked up three Hershey bars, a bag of chocolate-covered peanuts and a box of chocolate-dipped shortbreads.

She had to give the isoflavones something to do.

Dori paid for her groceries and declined the box boy's offer to take the single large bag out to her car.

This summer was about doing things for herself. And so far she was pleased with her progress.

She'd written ninety pages of what she estimated would be a book of 100,000 words, or four hundred pages. If she could find a way to keep her brothers in Europe, her father in a cast, and herself working at her current speed, she could be finished by the end of the summer.

She'd called a plumber about a leak in the downstairs bathroom faucet and had paid for the repairs. She'd watered the lawns and weeded the flower beds that surrounded the house. And she'd just spoken to a lawyer about getting Sal out of her life permanently.

She took a deep gulp of salty air as she stepped out of the market. Her life was on track. And it had only taken her the better part of twenty-six years.

She unlocked the door of her car and slid into her seat, the bag momentarily trapped between her chest and the steering wheel. She pushed up and sideways on the bag, managed to honk the horn, then leaned toward the passenger seat and deposited the bag.

She retrieved the blue corn chips and pulled the bag open. She put a chip between her teeth, her key in the ignition and started the car.

Yes, she thought. Her life was good. It was sort of a shame her brothers and her parents weren't here to see how she'd taken command of it. But if they were here, she'd be fighting for control of it—and probably losing.

So that would be counterproductive. She'd just have to be successful in silence.

She stopped the car at the parking lot's exit, looked both ways and pulled out onto Dancer Avenue.

The way her luck was running, she thought with pride, she should probably start planning her own autograph party. Nothing lavish—just a small champagne and gnoshes sort of thing, to which she would invite everyone who hadn't thought she had it in her.

Okay, now she was being a little too fanciful. She should probably try to find an agent or publisher first. Of course, if she got an agent, he'd want fifteen percent. But a publisher could take forever to respond to her if she *didn't* have an agent. It was a dilemma.

She should probably finish the book first, and then decide what to do.

She was startled by a loud sound of approbation from the back of the car. For an instant that seemed right—not at all unexpected. For all her family's interference in her life, there'd always been someone behind her encouraging her to "Go for it, Dori! Yeah!"

But she was alone in the car.

Her heart suddenly thumping, she looked into the rearview mirror, and saw... She stared, then blinked, then stared again. Could that be a cherubic little face looking back at her?

Her heart suddenly clogging her throat, she turned violently to the right, slammed on the brakes and brought her shuddering car to a stop on the narrow verge between the highway and the rocks rimming the cliffs outside Dancer's Beach.

The driver of a pickup behind her had to swerve to

avoid hitting her, and leaned on his horn to tell her what he thought of her driving.

"It's an angel," she told herself, half amazed, half terrified to look again. "My family couldn't be here so they've managed to hire a special guardian angel…"

Another sound of approbation came from the back seat.

One eye closed, Dori risked another look into the rearview mirror. She saw the smiling fat-cheeked little face again, then the waving of a pair of pudgy little arms. Then she heard a high-pitched squeal.

She unbuckled her belt and turned in her seat. Her jaw fell open as she looked into the velvety dark eyes of a baby strapped into a car seat.

The baby raised both arms again and squealed at her, smiling broadly.

"Holy sh—!" She stopped herself just in time. Just in case this *was* an angel.

Apparently unhappy with the sound of her voice, the cherub's smile disappeared, replaced by a pout, followed instantly by a scream of displeasure.

Dori leaped out of the car as traffic zoomed past, ran around to the other side and opened the door. Now thoroughly displeased with her reaction, the baby screwed his eyes closed, opened his mouth wide and blared his unhappiness to the world.

He was plump with thick dark hair sticking up in spikes. He wore blue denim rompers over a white T-shirt, and tiny little brown suede hiking books.

"Oh, my God!" Dori whispered, fussing with the car seat's protective bar. Her sisters-in-law all had babies and young children, and all the car seats worked in a slightly different way. "No, you don't work for Him, do you? You came to earth the normal way. You're a baby, not an angel. Or maybe an angel-baby."

Finally managing to raise the bar, she unbuckled the protective harness that held the still-screeching baby in place, then lifted him out of the seat. She rested him against her shoulder and patted his back. He felt hot and moist against her.

"Okay, sweetheart. It's okay, it's okay," she soothed, walking to the back of the car with him, pacing as she tried to figure out what on earth had happened. "Mommy must have accidentally put you in the wrong car," she said, then realized, even as the words came out of her mouth, that that couldn't have happened. She'd locked the car when she went into the market. Her brothers had drummed that safety precaution into her head.

And she had no car seat. Someone had installed it, then the baby, while she'd been in Coast Groceries. But how had someone gotten into her car?

Okay, okay, she told herself as she continued to walk back and forth, oblivious to the pale blue of the sky and the darker, sun-embroidered blue of the ocean. *Think. Stay calm. There's an explanation.*

Five minutes later, when the baby's wailing finally began to quiet down, all Dori could think of was that breaking into someone's car and installing a baby seat—and a baby—were deliberate acts. This hadn't been done by mistake.

This baby had been abandoned.

No. That didn't seem like quite the right word. *Abandoned* created images of a Dumpster or a doorstep. But someone had left this baby in an up-to-code car seat, probably aware that the owner of the car would be out shortly. Maybe they'd even watched from the bushes surrounding Coast Grocery's parking lot.

The baby stopped crying and, with a ragged little shudder, grabbed a fistful of Dori's shirt. He had Latino features, she thought, as he dropped his head on her shoulder.

She stood still and rocked him, wondering what to do now. The only sensible course of action would be to call the police. She had a cell phone in her purse.

But she made no move toward the car.

She loved having her arms full of a baby. She'd helped her brother Darrick when the twins had been left at the hospital right after birth and he'd thought they were his. In the past two years she'd taken care of the entire army of McKeon children at one time or another, and had longed for the day she'd add her own brood to the new generation.

But thanks to her own abandonment on her wedding day, that wasn't going to happen anytime soon.

She sighed and walked reluctantly toward the car, thinking of how this summer was supposed to be about proving herself capable and competent, and about finishing her book.

The baby might have been left in her car because of a squabble between his parents—one might have stolen him to hurt the other. His grandparents might be frantic, aunts or uncles worried.

At the car, she leaned into the back to put the baby back in the seat, resolving that she would drive back to town and the police station.

The baby screamed the minute she sat him down. Tears springing to her eyes, feeling like a monster, she buckled him in, secured the protective bar and backed out of the car to close the door.

That was when she noticed the diaper bag on the floor between the seats. It was bright blue-and-yellow plastic with elephants in party hats all over it. Two plastic baby bottles protruded from a compartment on the side, and a big front pocket bulged with something. She unzipped it to check, and found two disposable diapers.

A tiny pocket on the top flap yielded a pacifier, which she quickly offered to the baby. He took it in and began sucking, his screams turned off as though someone had flipped a switch.

Breathing a little sigh of relief, Dori unzipped the main compartment, hoping to find a note—any clue as to who the baby was and why he'd been left in her car.

And there it was, right on top, a piece of Garfield stationery folded in half. A very round handwriting filled the entire page.

"'Hi,'" she read aloud. "'This is Max. He's five-and-a-half months old and a very good baby. He's loving and cheerful. He wakes up a lot at night, but he'll fall asleep again when he sees your face.

'I love him, but I'm not a good mother. You don't know me, Dori, but you were once very kind to me, and I know you'll be kind to Max. Please don't take him to the police. The baby wipes will help you.

'Bless you.'"

Of course there was no signature.

"'You were once very kind to me,'" Dori repeated aloud, trying to remember. In Dancer's Beach, she wondered, or in Edenfield?

Since the baby'd been left here, she could only presume the act of kindness had taken place here. But what? When? She'd been raised to be kind, but she couldn't remember doing any good deed that would convince a woman to leave her her child!

She reread the note.

You don't know me. So it could have been an unconscious kindness she might never remember.

Please don't take him to the police.

She had to. It was illegal to simply pass children on to someone else like a hand-me-down.

She looked into Max's little face as she thought that, and he smiled at her around the pacifier, little arms and legs kicking with excitement at her recognition.

"All right," she said, rubbing a knuckle on his dimpled knee. "In your case, it's more like getting a precious gift than a hand-me-down. But I'm trying to prove something to my family this summer. Even to myself. That I can manage my life without everyone waiting around to lend a hand. And while I'd love to have you around, I'm afraid I'd consider you a handy excuse for not following through, you know?"

Max flailed and kicked again.

Dori rubbed his little knee and looked over the letter one more time, ready to fold it, put it back in the diaper bag, and take baby and bag to the police station.

The baby wipes will help you, she read again. That was a strange thing to write.

Dori dug past two baby outfits and a tiny blue knit sweater before she found the box of wipes. She opened it, wondering if Max's mother had stored in it tips on his care or a favorite toy.

She opened the lid—and stared in stupefaction at the contents of the box. Dead presidents! Grant! A three-inch stack of fifty-dollar bills filled the box.

With a gasp, she flipped through the stack and found that she was wrong. The bottom inch-and-a-half was Franklins! Hundred-dollar bills!

She quickly covered the box, looked around surreptitiously and, satisfied that everyone on the highway was traveling too fast to see what was going on in her car, stuffed it back under the baby clothes and zipped the bag shut.

With a comforting pat for the baby, she closed the back door, then ran around to slip in behind the wheel and lock all the doors. She sat for a moment, her breath caught in her lungs, which seemed to be refusing to do their job.

She made herself calm down. Draw in air, let it out. Breathe in, breathe out. In. Out. *There.* Oxygen was getting to her brain.

This wasn't so bad, after all, was it? Wasn't this just what she'd always wanted? A beautiful baby and enough cash to invest some and play with some. It wasn't an enormous fortune, but it was certainly enough to keep a single woman used to economizing, and a little baby.

She turned the key in the ignition and had to make a decision. Which way? Back to town and the police station? Or home?

McKeon morals flashed in her brain like a neon sign: YOU CANNOT KEEP THE MONEY.

"I know that," she told herself impatiently. "But, can I keep the baby?"

McKeon morals had nothing to offer in reply. They were ambivalent. The McKeons were a law-abiding family—but to the last person, they believed the good of their children came first.

Dori turned onto the highway, headed for home.

CHAPTER TWO

DORI FED MAX a baby food jar of weenies and beans she'd found in the bottom of the diaper bag. It was a task for which she should have had Olympic training.

The loving, cheerful baby was a horror when it came to dinner. He grabbed the spoon from her, and when she watched, thrilled that at such a tender age he wanted to feed himself, she got an eyeful of its contents.

He did not want to feed himself; he wanted to decorate. He flung the orangey-brown mixture all over the kitchen in a style reminiscent of Paul Klee. Within minutes, Dori herself was a breathing canvas.

After dinner, she bathed him in the downstairs bathroom in a baby tub left over from Dillon and Harper's little Danielle, now two years old. By the time it was over, there was no water in the tub, an inch on the floor, and Dori was soaked to the skin. At least she was no longer covered in weenies and beans.

For an hour afterward, she watched Max at play on a blanket she spread out in the middle of the living room floor. He was working his way across the blanket in a sort of swimming, arching movement that was surprisingly efficient. Up against the bottom of the sofa, his progress blocked, he stopped, clearly trying to decide what to do.

He braced himself on his arms and looked around for her. Spotting her, he gave her a gummy smile.

That was when a very scary notion occurred to her. He was absolutely beautiful, with a dark-eyed look that was very Latino. He reminded her of...Sal!

She stood up suddenly, startling the baby. She picked him up as he began to cry, turned him around, and put him down on the blanket again. He was quickly off in the other direction, looking like a little seal on the sand.

Sal! she thought. *Of course!* Was this Desideria's baby? Or some other woman's? She'd scoured the newspaper earlier for an item about a missing baby, for some little blurb in the police report. But there'd been nothing. And nothing on the six o'clock news.

Sal. That was a much more reasonable explanation than the idea that a complete stranger to whom she'd once been kind had left her a baby.

But what about the money?

Max yawned and began to rub his eyes. Dori picked him up and moved to the rocker in her parents' bedroom, which was off the living room. It was spacious, with wonderful wicker furniture and a deep wicker rocker that had lulled many McKeon babies to sleep.

Dori rocked and thought about the money. Seeing that much cash hidden at the bottom of a bag had made her jump to the conclusion that it had been stolen.

The baby wipes will help you, the note had said.

Maybe the cash had been put there as an attempt—albeit a faulty one—to pay her to care for Max.

It didn't seem quite like Sal to have stuffed cash into a diaper bag. He'd have opened a bank account and stashed a debit card with its PIN attached in the diaper bag.

Maybe Desi had done this without his knowledge. The note had definitely sounded as though it had been written by the baby's mother, not the father.

And she doubted that Sal was much for notes. She hadn't received so much as a postcard from him since the day a week after the wedding when he'd come to her apartment and she'd refused to see him. If he'd had something to say to her, he'd have done it directly and without subterfuge.

Still, this could very well be his baby.

Dori stroked the glossy dark head and felt Max slump against her as he finally gave in to sleep. She'd brought a portable crib down from upstairs and now put Max in it. She covered him with a well-used baby quilt that one of Harper's aunts had made for Darian. Its bright blues had faded with repeated washings, but the ducklings in each small square were snow white.

Dori breathed a small sigh of relief, unaware until that moment how tired she was. She went to the kitchen to retrieve the diaper bag, microwaved a cup of tea, and brought both back to the bedroom.

She closed the shade behind the sheer curtains then emptied the contents of the baby wipes box into the middle of the bed.

She counted $11,572. That was an odd amount.

Perhaps Desi had simply cleaned out a savings account.

Dori didn't want to feel sympathetic, so she tried to stop thinking about it. About Desideria, anyway. She put the money back in the box and hid the box in the bottom drawer of her parents' dresser.

She had to talk to Sal. She didn't want to, but she had to. If this was his baby and he didn't know about it, there'd be hell to pay for everyone when he found out.

She turned off the lights, locked up the house, took a shower with the door open so that she could listen for the baby, then went to bed. But she stared at the ceiling for two hours, unwilling to go to sleep for fear of having the wedding dream again. If she was going to have to deal civilly with Sal, she couldn't do it with the fresh anger the dream always left in her.

She was about to doze off, when Max awoke. She fed him, changed his diaper and rocked him until he went back to sleep. She put him in the crib and climbed back into bed, this time determined to get some sleep—whatever she dreamed about.

SAL DOMINGUEZ LOOKED over Dominguez Security's quarterly report and was surprised at what a profitable three months it had been. Seattle was full of homeowners and commercial clients concerned about making their premises impenetrable, concerned about the safety of their cars and their commercial fleets, and concerned about their own personal safety.

It was his good fortune that one of the first clients he'd served when he moved to town eighteen months ago had been a high-profile columnist for the *Post-Intelligencer* who'd offended a corrupt official and had needed a bodyguard. Though Sal had three other security agents, he'd taken the job himself.

He'd accompanied his client on a clandestine trip to the waterfront to retrieve vital documentation from a former aid to the official, when they'd been attacked by three men. Sal had sent one into the water, dispatched another after a brief altercation, then turned to see the third man draw a bead on his client, who was trapped in a corner.

Sal drew his own 9mm Smith & Wesson and fired as he ran toward his client, arriving just in time to take the third man's answering bullet in the shoulder as the man, too, went into the river.

The grateful columnist had had the forum through which to make sure word got around about Dominguez Security's dependability.

Sal handed the folder back to Diego Munoz, his vice president in charge of everything Sal didn't oversee—and his good friend. They'd met in Madre Maria when Sal was putting up the hospital and needed someone trustworthy and sufficiently obsessed with excellence to help him with the details.

By the time the hospital was up and running, they were friends, and Diego's wife, Manuela, was pregnant with their third child. It was no time to leave the man without employment. So, Sal had invited Diego to join him in the United States, where he'd open a security company.

Diego had the heart of an adventurer in a short, round body, and the sense of decorum of a butler. He was the one who'd insisted that the office look as if it belonged to a law firm rather than to a militia group.

He'd told Ben Richardson, a former wrestler, Los Angeles police officer, and now a bodyguard for Dominguez Security, to stop wearing camouflage on assignment.

"Unless you are guarding our client in a duck blind," Diego had said, "it is inappropriate."

Ben had taken offense, had turned to Sal for support, but had found none.

"He's right," Sal agreed. "Our clients go to the theater, the opera, fine hotels and restaurants, business meetings in important places. You function best if you don't stand out."

Ben had charged four three-piece suits to the company. Sal had paid for two.

"Excellent," Sal said now, leaning back in his chair. "We're in very good financial shape, and staffing's covered for the next two months. You and Manuela can take a vacation."

Diego, sitting stiffly in the client's chair, shook his head regretfully. "Miguel is on a baseball team, and Rosa is taking ballet lessons."

Sal envied the sparkle that came into Diego's eyes when he talked about his family. "Ballet lessons at four?" he asked in surprise.

Diego smiled. "She is a little butterball with the attitude of a lawn mower. We are hoping she will learn a little style."

Sal nodded. Perhaps that was what Dori lacked—ballet lessons. She was not a butterball, but she did have the attitude of a big-toothed, grass devouring, ride-on mower. He had to do something about her, he knew. He just didn't know what. And he seldom approached any task or brought on a confrontation until he knew he would emerge victorious.

Dori had so entangled things that no one could win at this point.

"Why don't *you* take a vacation?" Diego suggested.

Sal shook his head. "Where would I go?"

"Europe?" Diego suggested. "The Caribbean, the Mediterranean?"

"No. I have no desire to lay on a beach or to tour cathedrals."

"You're restless," Diego noted.

"I'm always restless." Sal grinned. "I need a twenty-story hotel filled with rich ladies with fine jewelry."

"Mmm. And what would you do when those ladies heard that a cat burglar was on the prowl and came to Dominguez Security for someone to protect them and their jewels?"

His grin widened. "Now, that's a profitable angle to the business I hadn't anticipated."

"As if you could steal."

"I *did* steal, Diego. I told you all about it."

"You gave everything to the village. You kept the school open, you got our goods to market, you put up the hospital."

"Duncan McKeon put up the money for the hospital."

"But you made it happen. Why are you so eager to dismiss your accomplishments?"

"Because at the bottom," he replied frankly, "I'm a really good thief. That's not precisely the legacy a man dreams of leaving."

Diego shook his head at him and stood. "You, *amigo,* need to see yourself through the eyes of a woman who loves you."

"Yes. Well. There is no such woman."

"There are many who would be willing."

"And they would flatter me in exchange for good sex and expensive baubles—but that's not what you're talking about, is it?"

"Good sex and expensive baubles?" a female voice repeated from the doorway. "I thought your business was alarms and bodyguards."

Sal leaned around Diego to see who was eavesdropping on their conversation. Had he not been as fit as his work required, he thought later, he might very well have died of a heart attack on the spot. Dori stood just inside his office.

She pointed into the hall. "I'm sorry for barging in. There's no one at the desk out there."

Diego, too, was speechless for a moment. Then he turned to Sal and said under his breath, "I've told you we should stagger lunch hours, but the girls like to go together and you let them. You will excuse me."

On his way out, he stopped and bowed stiffly in Dori's direction. He'd been her staunchest advocate before she'd left Sal. "It is nice to see you again, *Mrs. Dominguez.*" He emphasized her married name.

"And you, Diego," she said. "How are Manuela and the children?"

"They're well, thank you."

Sal had been so surprised by the sight of Dori's face, it wasn't until Diego touched the hand of the baby in her arms that he realized she wasn't alone.

He came around the desk, trying to strike an approach somewhere between collected and well-mannered. He found it hard to do, with his heart thudding against his ribs.

"Hello, Dori," he said, as she came toward him across the pale teal carpet. She wore white jeans and a simple rose-colored shirt. She'd cut her hair since they'd parted, and it was sticking up here and there and lay on her forehead in irregular wisps.

Her cheeks and her lips were the color of her shirt, and her eyes were dark and troubled, a curious overlay of anger snapping at him despite her courteous reply.

"Hello, Sal. I apologize if I interrupted a meeting."

"We were finished," Diego said, and left the office.

The baby in her arms smiled at Sal and waved his arms wildly. Sal felt a physical pain in his heart at the possibility the baby suggested. "And who's this?" he asked with pretended nonchalance.

"This is Max," she replied.

Max leaned away from her and stretched fat little arms toward him. Sal reached instinctively for him, unable to ignore the invitation.

"So, he *is* yours!" Dori said, anger now in her voice as well as her eyes.

Sal sat on the edge of his desk with the baby, not

certain what she was talking about. However, he had heard that tone before and it put him on the defensive.

"What do you mean?"

She sank into the chair Diego had just vacated. She looked tired as well as irritated. "I mean that he just reached for you as though he knows you."

"Knows me," he repeated, waiting for the words to make sense. "How could he know me? You just walked in with him."

She appeared off balance, uncertain. "He looks just like you," she said.

He looked into the baby's face, wondering what on earth Dori was trying to say. "He could be a Dominguez," he said, as the baby tried to remove his tie through his neck. "But if you recall," he said, peeling back little fingers to free himself, "I haven't been anywhere near you in two years."

"Well, what does that have to do with anything?" she demanded, coming to help disengage the little fingers. "*I'm* not his mother."

"Then what are you doing with him?"

"Desideria put him in my car!" she said loudly, backing up with the baby, who was now screaming.

"Desi..." he began, mystified. He unfastened the tie and yanked it off, then took the baby back. Max stopped crying instantly. Sal felt a definite satisfaction that he didn't bother to hide. "Will you please sit down and try to make sense. What do you mean, Desi left the baby in your car? Where? You've been to Tucson?"

Dori fell into the chair, the tie held in her two hands

as though she intended to garrote someone with it. "Tucson?" she repeated.

Sal nodded, quickly pushing his blotter away before the baby dragged toward him a variety of office supplies he could either choke on or use to ruin everything else on the desk. "She lives there with her husband."

"I thought her husband went to jail."

"This is a new husband."

Dori swallowed and seemed to collapse in upon herself. "You're sure?"

"I'm sure," he replied. "I flew there last weekend for Guadalupe's baptism."

She groaned and dropped both arms over the sides of the chair. "Well, damn," she said.

DORI TRIED TO THINK, but she was finding it difficult with Salvatore Dominguez a mere four feet away from her. He was still handsome, still had that calm assurance that made her feel innocent and incompetent. And he handled Max with easy confidence, though she knew he didn't have much experience with babies. At least, he hadn't two years ago.

And he was telling her he *wasn't* Max's father?

She was exhausted and confused. "I thought you and Desideria had a..." She wriggled her fingertips in explanation. His eyes went to her hands, then to her eyes. This was bringing them back to two years ago, and she didn't want to go there.

"A what?" he asked, his easy good humor changing suddenly.

The perceptive baby detected it and looked up at

him. Sal smiled and pinched the baby's chin. Max laughed delightedly.

"A relationship," Dori replied.

He glanced at her but kept an eye on the baby's hands as they explored his watch. "We did. But it was not a sexual one. You'd have known that if you'd waited for me to explain."

"You're the one who left," she said, struggling to keep her voice down.

"I asked you to wait for my return."

"I came almost four thousand miles," she said, fighting for composure, "to tell you that I loved you. And you left me on our wedding day—not two minutes after the ceremony—to take care of someone else!"

"I asked Diego to explain, but he told me you refused to listen. You packed your things and flew home."

"I didn't want Diego," she said loudly. "I wanted you. I searched my soul and came all that way to find you!"

The baby moved on to study Sal's fingers. Dori noticed for the first time that Sal wore a wedding ring.

Something cold and hard rose to the middle of her chest and felt as though it cut off her air. "You're married," she said in a strangled voice.

He glanced up at her again, surprised by that observation. "To you," he said. Then, realizing that her eyes were on his ring, he added, "You gave this to me, remember?"

His eyes went to her left hand: it was naked. Brutally, she held it up for him to see.

"Well, I am not. We had a ceremony, but immediately after that the groom left. We never shared a bed or did any of the things that make a couple truly married."

"We repeated the vows," he pointed out.

She made a scornful sound. "Which you broke two minutes later. Hardly cause for me to consider myself Dori Dominguez."

"I came back to find you gone," he countered. "You're the one who decided you didn't want to be married, after all."

"I doubt anyone would be surprised about that, if they knew."

The look in his eyes disputed that. "You might be surprised," he said, "if you admitted your real reasons to yourself."

"What?" she demanded.

Max made a sudden grab for a letter opener that should have been out of reach. Sal pushed it farther away, then turned Max around and stood him on the desk. "This child will make a good outfielder one day. His arms are expandable."

"You're ignoring my question," Dori said.

Sal nodded. "That line of conversation never gets us anywhere. Let's forget that for the moment, and tell me about Max being left in your car."

She *wanted* to pursue "that line of conversation." She'd driven six hours into Seattle and its horrible traffic, certain she had a case against Sal's old girlfriend, only to learn that she might be mistaken about their relationship. Not that it mattered. He'd still gone to Desideria the day he'd married Dori.

But, damn it, something inside her still responded to him in the same old way.

Then she noticed a photo on his desk. She remembered when he'd taken it, just two days before their wedding. Dori was pictured seated on his veranda, relaxed in a high-back chair, smiling. Clearly in love.

She wanted to run, but that was not the way to prove herself capable and competent.

With a sigh, she explained about the trip to the grocery store and the surprise she got on the way home.

"Someone broke into your car?" he asked with a frown.

She nodded. "Nothing was taken, just—" she indicated the baby "—deposited." She handed him the note.

She saw him read it quickly, then read it over more slowly. "A child's hand," he said. "What act of kindness did you do her?"

Dori shrugged. "I don't remember anything particular. Like most people, I try not to be *un*kind."

He glanced up from the note in dry amusement. "Unless, of course, you're dealing with me."

She let that pass.

"What does she mean about the box of wipes?" he asked. "What kind of help?"

She realized she'd been so involved with the baby and their argument that she'd forgotten one of the more intriguing parts of the mystery. She reached into the diaper bag for the box, then stood and handed it across the desk.

Sal opened it and stared at it a moment, while Max was fascinated by a drawer pull.

"It's $11,572," Dori said. "I guess whoever left me the baby, left the money to help me take care of it. I was going to give it back to you or have you give it to Desi. But if it was neither of you..." She shrugged, unsure where to go from there. "Who do I give it to? If I take it to the police, I'll have to explain about the baby—and they'll take him away."

Sal frowned at the money, apparently thinking.

"Maybe I'll just wait," she went on, "and see what happens. It might turn up in the news. Dancer's Beach is a small town. There might be gossip about a theft or missing money. Then I can sneak it back to whoever lost it."

Sal gave her a quick look that was a clear negative. "No," he said, as though the look hadn't been clear enough. "You've obviously been watched and followed, if someone knows your name and waited for you to go into the grocery store before putting the baby in the car. Someone broke into your car and left you a suspiciously large amount of cash. This is not the behavior of a person on the right side of the law."

"I know," she said defensively. "But I don't think anyone intended me harm. I mean—"

"You may be right," he interrupted. "But what concerns me is where this money came from. It isn't wrapped as though it came from a bank. The way the bills are organized, largest to smallest, it looks like it may have been someone's bank deposit."

"You mean a business?"

"Maybe. Or a bookie, or a drug dealer..."

"In Dancer's Beach?"

"Bookies and drug dealers," he said patiently, "are everywhere. And you don't know where this person came from, do you?"

"No."

"What if a desperate woman stole this money from her drug-dealing boyfriend, or her pimp? And he comes looking for it?"

She folded her arms stubbornly. He was right, but this summer was about... She knew what it was about. She didn't have to tell herself again. "If that happens, I can take care of myself."

"And the baby?"

That gave her pause. She'd taken self-defense courses. She could handle a mugger if she could see him coming. But if he took her by surprise, she had a tendency to hyperventilate and pass out cold.

She might be willing to risk herself, but Max?

Sal stood, transferring the baby to his hip. Max had his telephone receiver.

"Diego!" Sal shouted.

Diego appeared in the doorway. He always reminded Dori of a very sweet undertaker.

"Yes?" Diego asked.

"I'm going on vacation, after all," Sal said.

CHAPTER THREE

"WAIT A MINUTE." Dori stood, her chin at a stubborn angle. "You're not thinking you're coming home with me?"

"No." She looked relieved. He strode toward the door with the baby. "I *am* coming home with you." He enjoyed another glimmer of satisfaction at her annoyed surprise. "Will you bring the bag, please?"

She'd started to follow him, sputtering, then turned back to grab the diaper bag off the floor and sling it over her shoulder. "Sal, you're not coming home with me," she said, running to keep up with him, then colliding with his back when he stopped to talk to his secretary, who was just returning from lunch. "I'm writing a book this summer. I don't have time for continual arguments. And where do you think you're going to stay?"

Claudette Bingham, a tall, slender redhead with a photographic memory and a quiet nature that made even Sal seem frantic, had been with Dominguez Security since the day he had opened the doors.

She smiled at the baby in his arms and blinked at Dori. "*Mrs.* Dominguez?" she asked.

Dori put a hand to her forehead, "No, I..." she began hotly, then, apparently realizing the confusion wasn't Claudie's fault, drew a breath and started again. "Technically, yes. Actually, no."

Claudie raised an eyebrow at Sal.

"Don't worry," he said, bending over her desk to make a note on the calendar there. Max leaned out of his arms and reached for the large paper cup Claudie had just placed there. "We don't understand it, either."

She took the cup from Max and put the straw to his lips. "Can he have a drink?" she asked Dori. "It's juice."

"Sure," Dori said defeatedly. "Sal, we—"

"This man's name is in the file," he said, pointing with the tip of his pen to the name he'd written. "There are two addresses for him. I'll be at the one at Dancer's Beach. You can reach me there or on my cell."

"How long will you be gone?" Claudie asked, smiling as Max drank greedily.

"I'm not sure. We have a case I've decided to handle myself."

"We're not a *case,*" Dori said. "I didn't come here to hire you, I came to ask you...Sal, no way!" She'd been reading Claudie's calendar upside down and suddenly realized he'd written her brother Duncan's name on it. "You are *not* staying at my brother's house in Dancer's Beach. *I'm* staying there."

Sal pulled a ring of keys out of his pocket and held up the one with the signature star bauble attached to all the keys to the McKeon residence. "I've been invited to use it any time I please."

"Well, presumably he meant when the house was empty. It's not empty now."

There was a loud noise as Max struck bottom in the cup. "All gone!" Claudie said and tossed the cup away.

Max protested with a shriek. Sal handed him to Claudie. "Would you watch him for a few minutes, please?"

"Of course. Come here, big boy."

Alissa, Diego's secretary, and Bianca, who kept the master schedule, all crowded around her desk.

Sal took Dori's arm and drew her into a small conference room at the far end of the hall. It had gray-and-burgundy padded chairs around an oval mahogany table, and formal burgundy drapes. Clients talking security seemed to relax here. He hoped the atmosphere would do the same for Dori.

"What do you think I intend in going home with you?" he asked. It always surprised her when an argument was placed in her lap. With three older brothers, she was used to having to fight even to be noticed, much less included. Sal wondered just how far that chin could angle up.

"You want to try to get back together," she said defensively.

He had to look into her eyes to spare himself the vision of neat little breasts covered in pink, of slender hips with just enough sway to them to be seductive, of graceful legs. Images of her had haunted his dreams—waking and sleeping—for two years.

He walked away from her toward the window, because now he was going to lie through his teeth. "If that was what I wanted," he said, "wouldn't I have tried to do that sometime over the past two years?" It *had* been what he'd wanted, but he'd had to make sure he had the business in order first. Then he'd waited for the right moment. And here it was.

There was a moment's silence as he stared out the window. He guessed he'd hurt her feelings. Perversely, she claimed to want nothing to do with him, but was probably upset that he'd suggested he wanted nothing to do with her. That was Dori.

"You didn't know where I was," she said finally.

"You went back to your apartment for a month after the wedding," he said, turning to sit on the edge of the deep windowsill. She stood and watched him from the side of the room, her arm resting on the curved back of one of the chairs. "You went back to England for research from August to November. You came home for the holidays. You spent Thanksgiving at your parents, where all the family collected. You joined the family at the summer house for two weeks over the Christmas holidays. Then you took a teaching job at Edenfield High during the second half of the year and were hired for the following year." Again, she was surprised. "I've known where you were every moment."

He couldn't tell what she thought of that. She folded her arms and asked calmly, "If you've known where I was, why didn't you serve me with divorce papers?"

"Because you're the one who wants the divorce," he reminded her. "Not I."

"Yet you haven't tried to change my mind."

He shrugged. "I know you to be a stubborn woman who wants things her way. My standing on my head to make you see things differently isn't going to help. I'm waiting for the day you come to your senses."

That nudged her temper. He'd known it would. Her anger was almost easier on him than that lost look that had come over her when she'd realized he'd known her every move over the past two years, yet had never approached her.

"I am being sensible," she said, dropping her arm from the chair and walking away from him. "What woman wants to be married to a man who runs out on their wedding day?"

"Then why didn't *you* file for divorce?"

"Because…"

There was a struggle in her eyes that she tried desperately to hide. If he hadn't once understood every subtlety in her, he'd have missed it.

"Because I didn't have the money," she said with sudden resolution. "But now I have, and I've hired a lawyer."

Now he knew he was the one struggling not to look desperate. "Then, there's nothing to worry about. In all this time, I've made no effort to reconcile, and you've started divorce proceedings. So there's little emotional danger if we spend time together in the same house for the sake of your safety and that of the baby."

She didn't look convinced.

"I'm Mexican, Dori," he said, getting up from the sill and going toward her. "Where I come from, women are buxom and warm with inviting eyes and smiling lips. They're not always sniping and turning away. Believe me. I have no desire to reignite an old flame.''

She maintained her cocked-chin hauteur, but he couldn't tell if that was pain in her eyes. She turned away from him toward the door, her manner unhurried, but possibly...injured.

"But I don't want to see you in danger, either," he said briskly, reaching around her to grasp the doorknob. "Nor the baby. So let me keep you safe while we get to the bottom of this," he bargained. "Then your lawyer can prepare the divorce papers."

She turned to him. With his hand on the doorknob, they were mere inches apart, and history returned in a rush. Every stirring he'd ever had for her when they'd been meeting about Julie; every hot desire that had blistered the night they'd spent together during what her family now referred to as "the Julie incident," every dark and lonely moment since he'd yearned for even the scent of her—all rose up to pulse between them and make a mockery of his denial.

His impulse was to cup her head in his hand and kiss her senseless. But there was more at stake at this moment.

"Doesn't that make sense?"

She looked into his eyes. He had no idea whether she was seeing the logical reason that supported his Machiavellian plan, or the lust that had almost overcome it.

"Yes," she said finally. "It does."

He opened the door, trying not to betray his enormous relief. "Good," he said.

"I'm not cooking for you," she warned.
"I appreciate that," he replied.

DORI THOUGHT HER CAR seemed crowded with Sal in the passenger seat of her little red import. He drove an American luxury car, and she'd followed him from his office to his condo where he'd packed a suitcase and collected his laptop.

"You still drive like a wild woman," he said, though he appeared relaxed enough. "If you're going to be a mother, you're going to have to get that inclination under control."

She did like to drive—and the faster the better. Washington traffic encouraged her to indulge that habit. Everything else in her life—school, the Georgian women who so fascinated her, her family who were always watching— required that she be orderly, careful, controlled.

But pushing her foot down on the accelerator and controlling the maneuverable little car made her feel reckless, yet still in charge. And she liked that.

"You're safe," she told him with a quick side glance.

She caught his answering look. It told her he wasn't so sure. But he watched the traffic with no apparent concern. He didn't even make a sudden move of alarm when a truck cut in front of her to catch the freeway exit, and she had to slam on the brakes, then change lanes so the car behind them didn't drive over them.

Maybe, she thought, that doubtful glance wasn't

referring to her driving. Maybe she made him feel unsafe in other ways.

No. He'd just told her in no uncertain terms that he no longer had feelings for her. And that was best. She was moving on this summer.

She glanced in the rearview mirror and saw Max sound asleep in his seat.

"I noticed that your accent seems less pronounced," she observed, remembering how his soft, round pronunciations and his elegantly constructed sentences had fascinated her.

"I issue a lot of instructions and orders on the phone and the radio in my work," he explained. "So I've been concentrating on making sure I'm understood."

A good point, she had to agree, but he sounded so...American.

The traffic thinned south of Olympia, but the road was dominated by large trucks; she had to pay close attention to the traffic.

They stopped for dinner in Longview, just across the river from Oregon. Max was refreshed by his long nap and drummed a discordant tune with a spoon on the tray of his high chair. Dori realized that she'd been driving all day long on four hours' sleep.

The helpful waitress brought a package of crackers to quiet the baby. "Bless you!" Dori said, opened the package, and broke off a small bite. Max took it in the palm of his hand and shoved it into his chin. His groping little mouth finally found it, and he chewed triumphantly.

"You're sure you want to do this?" Sal asked, as Dori offered Max another bite.

"Do what?" she asked.

"Raise a baby."

She was surprised by the question. "Of course I'm sure."

"Because your brothers all have families and you have to keep up, just like when you were children?"

Yesterday that question might have offended her, but she'd thought about it on the drive to Seattle and now it only amused her. "I don't think so. They left me behind ages ago when they all embarked upon successful and dynamic careers. No, Max is just for me. Or maybe for him. When I first discovered him in the back of my car, it took him a couple of minutes to calm down, but then he just melted against me—almost as though he was home. And that's how he felt to me. At last I was holding what I've always wanted."

Sal looked a little concerned. "But you look exhausted. Did you get any sleep last night?"

"Four hours," she answered. The waitress placed a burger and fries in front of Dori, and a Reuben and soup before Sal. "The exhausting part was driving in Washington. I don't know how you do that every day." She peppered her French fries and handed him the shaker.

Max studied their plates and stirred anxiously in his highchair. Dori took several small pieces of bun off her burger and put them on his tray. He began the laborious but clearly interesting process of getting them from tray to mouth.

"I'm used to it now. It hones both my killer and my protective instincts. Will you give up teaching because of the baby?"

She'd thought about that, too. "I don't think I'll be able to. Even if I sell my book, it'll have limited appeal, so I won't make enough to quit my job. But it'll probably pay for day care."

"How close are you to finishing the book?"

"Not very close. I've finished about a quarter of it, but it's going well." She dipped a French fry in the side of blue cheese dressing she'd ordered. "But you know, while I was driving up, I was also thinking that if I made some changes, I could turn it into a work of fiction and potentially make it more salable."

"Change a scholarly work to fiction?"

"Yes. It was supposed to be a book about how the personalities of the women of the period were affected by their clothing, their surroundings, and the very little that was expected of them besides attracting a man and bearing his children."

A quarter of Sal's sandwich was already gone. He waggled his eyebrows over the rim of his coffee cup. "My ideal of womanhood," he said, putting the cup down. "Go on."

He was remarkably easy to talk to, she realized, now that they'd decided they wanted nothing to do with one another. She suddenly felt more free than she had in the past two years. It was amazing.

"What if I made the heroine a seamstress of the period," she explained, "who'd always wanted to be a doctor or a lawyer or someone powerful. But she has to make her living in one of the few careers acceptable for women, dressing other women to help them attract men. She does so in the hope that those men will ultimately get her the things she wants. Until the women start dying and she's always the last person they've seen before they're killed.''

"Did she do it?"

"No."

"Then, who?"

"I don't know."

He arched an eyebrow. "Isn't that a major problem for completion of the project?"

She laughed. "Well, yes. But I'm feeling very enthused about it, and thinking that as I work along I'll come to a solution." Then she sighed ruefully as Max, finished with his pieces of bread, screamed again. "Though how I'll accomplish that with Mighty Mouth, here, I'm not sure."

"I'll watch him," Sal said, "for as long as I'm at the house."

She turned to him suspiciously, not entirely sure what to say. It was a generous offer, but she couldn't stop wondering if he had an ulterior motive.

"What?" Sal asked with a half laugh. "Are you going to second-guess my every effort to help you? I thought we had come to an agreement."

"We have," she said, her tone subdued. "I'm just a little surprised that you *want* to help me."

"I'm thinking of you as a client."

That made her a little nervous. "How much am I paying you?"

"A no-charge client. We do that once in a while,

if someone's in danger because they've stood up for something we believe in."

"But I haven't done that."

He pointed to Max. "You're looking out for a helpless baby. So, try to relax about this. I'll watch him part of the time so you can work, and you can spell me once in a while so I can explore Dancer's Beach. Julie's always telling me how much she loves it there."

"All right." His help would make a big difference to her ability to meet her goals for the summer. She was a little confused by it, despite his reassurances, but she would keep those concerns to herself.

"How is it that you're so good with babies?" she asked.

"Diego's children," he replied. "I've taken care of them for him and Manuela quite a few times. Delia, the baby, is just a year old."

"I see." So he would be an asset with Max. "Did I mention that I'm not cooking for you?" she teased.

"You did." He picked up the second half of his sandwich. "And I can only interpret that to mean that you do have some regard for me after all. I'll cook. You used to like my *frijoles* with chorizo and cheese, as I recall."

She'd stayed in his small rancho outside Madre Maria for almost a week before they were married. She'd worked with him at the hospital every day, and he'd cooked for her every night. Happy moments from that time rushed back to her, complete with the aromas and flavors of his kitchen.

"But none of that napalm-bomb salsa." She

laughed. "You have to tone it down a little. And easy on the chipotle peppers in the chili."

"Sissy *gringa,*" he taunted. "All right. I'll take it easy on the hot stuff."

Their eyes met and held as they shared the happy memories of those few precious days. And for one breathless moment, when she seemed to see all the way into his heart, she had a premonition that she was making a terrible mistake.

Then the shock of his defection and the long, lonely days that followed came back to her as well, and she knew she'd never be able to forgive and forget that. There was no danger here that she might fall in love again.

"Good," she said with sudden coolness. "Because that chili the night Diego and Manuela came made me sick."

"Three bowls of chili," he said, apparently aware that she was putting a damper on their memories, "on top of three margaritas, would make anybody sick."

She'd been deliriously happy and filled with the spirit of celebration, as she recalled, but she didn't want to admit that so she dropped the subject.

"I'll drive the rest of the way," he said, taking the keys from her as they walked across the parking lot to the car. Max, in his arms, made a grab for the keys and shrieked when Sal held them away.

"Our lives would be simpler," Sal said, unlocking the car with the remote as they approached, "if we tied his arms to his body."

Dori opened the back door behind the passenger

side and took Max, then placed him in his car seat. "I know. He's like an octopus with extenders."

Max went peacefully, yawning as she strapped him in and lowered the bar.

Dori climbed into the passenger seat, finding it strange. She was seldom a passenger anymore, and the vantage point felt odd.

"Can I back-seat drive?" she asked, buckling her belt.

Sal put the key in the ignition and grinned at her over his arm. "The way you drive, I don't think it would be fair to tell *me* how."

She made a face. "Duncan taught me. I think the style comes from trying to outrun the paparazzi."

She fell asleep somewhere along the Columbia River, heading for Astoria, and didn't awaken until he stopped for gas somewhere south of Cannon Beach—still a good hour-and-a-half from Dancer's Beach.

"Want me to take over?" she asked, stretching her arms out ahead of her.

"No, thank you," Sal replied. "The road is quiet."

Dori suddenly remembered the baby, and turned in her seat to see him fast asleep, his head slumped to his left side. She unbuckled her belt, kneeled on her seat to turn around and tucked his blanket around him.

"Are you cold?" Sal asked, as she settled down again. "Manuela always puts a blanket on the baby when *she's* cold."

"When the baby can't tell you," she said, rubbing her arms in the sleeveless shirt, "how you feel is your only way to judge. It was such a beautiful summer day, I stupidly didn't think about a sweater."

Sal turned up the heat and reached behind his seat with his right hand, carefully watching the road. "I threw one back here somewhere. Ah. Here it is—" He produced it and put it in her lap.

It was a V-neck pullover in his favorite black—a throwback, he'd once told her, to his days as a thief. She pulled it on, catching a faint whiff of something subtle and herbal.

"Ooh." She couldn't help the expression of pleasure as she pushed her arms into the soft sleeves. "Cashmere?"

"Yes," he replied. "A gift from Diego and Manuela last Christmas. Warmer?"

"Yes, thank you." She reached into the glove compartment, remembering suddenly the Hershey with almonds she'd stashed there that morning. She unwrapped it, snapped it in half and handed half to Sal.

"What is it?" he asked, taking it from her.

"Chocolate," she replied. She bit off a chunk and let the delicious sweet melt on her tongue.

She heard his strong teeth snap off a piece.

"You still have that sweet tooth," he observed.

"I do." She took another bite and rested her head on the back of the seat. "Do you still make flan with that wonderful Mexican vanilla?"

"I can put it on the menu," he replied.

"I'll bet Max will love it."

"If you're willing to share."

"You could just double the batch."

"I'll consider that."

The chocolate made her feel, temporarily at least, that all was well with the world. The delicious soft sweater awakened the latent hedonist in her. She curled up, leaned against the door and was asleep in a matter of seconds.

SAL HAD A VAGUE MEMORY of the route to the McKeons' summer home, from his one and only visit there after he'd broken up the Cat Pack in Florida. While he was the McKeon's guest for several days, he and Dori had spent hours walking the beach and talking—and as usually happened when they talked, getting nowhere.

He'd proposed, tired of trying to make sense of their relationship and determined to simply let it have life. He was the kind of man who made things happen his way; he'd had to be. A life of poverty was not a happy prospect for the future, so he had changed things.

Dori, however, had dealt her entire life with older brothers who insisted she do what they considered to be in her best interest. Sal knew she didn't fully understand to this day that what governed her brothers was the notion that she was special, not that she was incompetent. A little sister in their lives, particularly after the loss of their brother Donovan, had given them a cause for the protective masculinity developing within them.

As they'd grown older, and she'd grown more beautiful, more intelligent, more eager to escape their continued protection, they'd become even more vigilant.

Dori, therefore, resisted everything and everyone who presented a threat to her independence. And Sal thought the idea of marriage had done just that.

He'd gone home to Mexico with the funds Duncan had given him for the hospital, certain Dori would miss him and be right behind him.

But it had taken her a year of soul-searching to finally decide that being without him was worse than being with him. He remembered his excitement at the sight of her, his hope that finally he would have the family he wanted.

He remembered their wedding day and how beautiful she had looked as the sun filtered through her mantilla. Her eyes had been filled with love for him and her hands had been on his arm, his shoulder, as though she had to touch him to exist.

And he'd known that at long last, after all the control he'd exerted time and again to leave her untouched, she would finally be his. He could see them in his imagination, body to body in his bed, making love as he'd known they would from the first time he ever saw her.

Then his friends had burst into the church, right after the ceremony, with the news of Desi's husband—and everything had taken a sorry, sorry turn.

It had been a terrible thing to leave Dori, but had he not gone, Desi would be dead today. He'd gone to Dori after Paco had been returned to jail, and had tried to explain that to her, but she hadn't wanted to listen.

Finally, disappointed in her and angry at himself as well as at her, he went back to Madre Maria to finish the addition to the hospital. He'd expected to hear every day that she'd filed for divorce, but that news never came.

And then she'd shown up at his office this afternoon. Now their relationship had come full circle to the house in Dancer's Beach.

He passed the welcome sign and followed the highway to the road that turned up the hill. He was afraid he might not recognize the street in the darkness, but she'd left the porch lights on, and he saw the white farmhouse with its window boxes, front porch furniture and decorative columns backlit by the old Georgian coach lamps on either side of the front door.

He guided the car into the driveway, turning off the motor as he drew close to the garage.

He gave Dori a gentle nudge. "We're home, *querida*," he said.

She emitted a soft little groan and, eyes still closed, turned toward him, arms unfolding to reach for him.

He remained still for a heartbeat, realizing she must still be ensnared by some dream that put that soft smile on her lips.

"Salvatore," she breathed with a little pout. "Come to me. It's been so long."

His breath left him, and he couldn't think. He shouldn't let this happen after what he'd promised, but he couldn't imagine why not.

He leaned toward her, and her smile widened as one of her hands went into his hair and the fingertips of the other explored the line of his jaw.

"Tonight, my love," she whispered, eyelashes fluttering. "Tonight at last!"

His temperature rose ten degrees when her lips

parted and she leaned even closer. He knew he shouldn't do this, that he should wake her, but he simply didn't have the moral fiber. He opened his mouth over hers and let her have full rein.

Her tongue explored his, ran along his bottom lip, touched his teeth, then her lips moved on his with cleverness and ingenuity.

In silence, he responded with all the ardor she inspired. He kissed her throat as she nibbled at his ear, kissed her chin as she kissed his eyelids, and finally, in danger of really making this the night she saw in her dream, he tried to catch a fistful of her hair and pull her back, but her hair was now cut too short.

She woke up with a suddenness that startled both of them.

He watched the expression in her eyes change from languid desire to startled awareness to molten anger.

"Sal!" she said in accusation, pushing against him.

He caught her wrists and tried to be reasonable despite his disappointment. "Whoa. Think a minute. You were dreaming."

She looked around, and then he felt the tension leave her. "You beckoned me," he said, feeling obligated to explain. "You put your arms—"

"I know, I know," she said, pulling free of him. "It was my dream, after all," she added with a sigh. "I'm sorry."

He shouldn't say it, but he did anyway. "I'm not."

Even in the darkness, he could see the troubled look in her eyes.

"It was just a dream," she insisted, her voice a little rough.

He nodded. He could tell by the way she'd reached for him that it was the same dream *he'd* lived on for two years.

But she wouldn't want to hear that.

"Right," he said, reaching across her to push open her car door. "And we had a deal."

"I'm sorry if I...upset you."

She looked a little stricken, guilty. Upset him. Major understatement.

"Not a problem," he said, pushing his own door open. "You have a long history of upsetting me. It's a comfort that some things never change."

CHAPTER FOUR

TROUBLE STARTED right away. Dori took Max inside, hoping he would remain asleep. She was exhausted and troubled and thinking gloomily that she'd finally gotten the wedding dream to work out the way she'd wanted it to—the two of them going back to his rancho to finally make love—only to be awakened by rude reality before getting to the good part.

And now he probably thought she had designs on him, after all.

She carried Max into the downstairs bedroom that she'd been using and lay him in the crib.

"I would prefer that you and the baby sleep upstairs," Sal said from the bedroom doorway. "I'll sleep down here."

"Why?" she asked.

"Because you're out of the way, if anything happens."

She pointed to the crib and her small desk. "But the crib's down here and my—"

He cut her off with a nod, handing her the laptop off the desk, then picking up the small oak piece. "They're easily moved." And he carried it toward the stairs as he spoke. "I know you once occupied the attic room, but the stairs are too hard to manage with the baby. Which of the second-floor rooms do you want?"

She followed him as far as the stairs off the kitchen. "I was happy down here."

He went on up the stairs. "I'll pick one, then."

"Dillon's," she called after him, after a small growl of exasperation, "overlooking the garden. First one on the right."

A loud yowl came from the direction of the crib. She hurried back to find Max braced on his arms and smiling. He was not upset, simply vocalizing. And very wide awake.

Great.

As Sal carried the crib upstairs, Dori followed with the baby, thinking grumpily that only thirty-six hours ago she'd been congratulating herself on how well the summer was going. Now, a brief day-and-a-half later, she found herself in possession of a baby, eleven-thousand dollars and some change, the husband she hadn't seen in two years, and a headache so bad it was probably registering on a Richter scale somewhere. Another Dorianne success story.

Sal had placed her desk near the window, and the baby's crib in a dark corner of the room, leaving her nothing to complain about. "Thank you," she said stiffly.

Sal headed for the door. "I'll bring your clothes up," he said.

"No." She pointed to the room's tiny closet, packed with summer clothes and toys that stayed here when Dillon, Harper and the children went home. "There won't be any place to put them."

He leaned against the doorway. "Would one of the other rooms have worked better?"

"Same kind of closets. I'll manage."

"All right." He came toward her, beckoning to Max, who almost leaned out of her arms toward Sal. "I'll get him back to sleep. You go to bed."

She turned away with the baby, who protested. "I slept most of the way home while you drove. You go to bed, and I'll get him back to sleep."

"Dori, why don't you—?" he began.

"You're here to protect us from crooks," she snapped at him, "not to save us from insomnia."

He raised both hands in a gesture of surrender. "All right. I'll get you the diaper bag."

She wanted to tell him she'd get it herself, but that would have been petty. She felt petty enough to do it, anyway, but Max was now screaming in her ear and demanding her full attention.

She paced the upstairs hall with him, wondering what had happened to his pacifier. It was somewhere in the back seat of the car, probably lost when he fell asleep in his seat.

She started for the stairs, not relishing the idea of searching for the pacifier with a screaming baby, when Sal reappeared with the diaper bag—and the pacifier.

"I noticed this," he said, handing it to her, "when I went back to the car to make sure I'd locked it. I rinsed it under the hot water downstairs." He walked around her and took the diaper bag into Dillon's room.

She offered Max the pacifier, and he took it eagerly. Blessed silence filled the hallway.

Sal emerged from Dillon's room, and they faced each other, several feet apart.

"Got everything you need?" he asked.

"Yes," she said, the silence suddenly deafening. She felt her entire body calm down a notch. She was even able to smile. "Thank you."

"Sure. What time do you want breakfast in the morning?"

"I'm usually up at seven. But there isn't much in the kitchen. I'll have to go shopping."

"I'll find something for breakfast. We can go shopping after you get your writing time in tomorrow. We'll need some things for Max, too, I imagine. Clothes, diapers, toys."

"Yes. Well." The corridor seemed to narrow as she walked past him to the bedroom. The warm air upstairs was growing heavy and humid. She had room to move, but it was as though she'd lost control of her body and something was pushing her toward him, and him toward her.

Suddenly she had a vivid picture of the very end of her dream. Of Sal and her in the middle of his bed, their arms around each other as they lay body to body, the knowledge that they would finally have each other intoxicating and thrilling.

Having to force herself, she moved past him and into the room. "Thanks for bringing everything up," she said abruptly. "We'll try not to keep you awake." And she closed the door.

The breath left her in a long, slow, slither of sound.

Max now leaned against her, eyes heavy. She sat on the edge of her bed and rocked him, wondering how she was going to survive cohabitation with Sal. It had been less than an hour, and she was already prepared to throw in the towel.

She just needed a good night's sleep, she told herself bracingly. Max was opposed to that, of course, but if she could manage to rest between early-morning bouts of wakefulness, she would see things more clearly tomorrow.

Max was fast asleep in half an hour. She put him in the crib, then peeled down to her underwear and climbed into Dillon's and Harper's bed. She was asleep in minutes.

Max woke at two. Dori pulled on her shirt and wrapped Max in his blanket to take him downstairs with her while she filled a bottle. But they were intercepted by Sal, standing on the top stair with a plastic baby bottle shaped like a bear. He wore jogging shorts and a T-shirt.

She tried not to stare at the cotton pulled tightly across his shoulders. He seemed to be avoiding looking at her legs.

"I heard him," he said, "and remembered that everything was downstairs. I'm sorry it's all so inconvenient, but you're safer up here."

She couldn't help the smile. "If you keep acting as my personal servant, it'll be no problem."

He smiled, too. "I'm happy to fill that role—to a point."

"Oh, now," she teased, "if you're going to put qualifications on it, it won't work."

He handed her the bottle with a grin. "We'll discuss terms in the morning," he said, and ran lightly down the stairs again.

Dori put Max back to bed with his bottle, then went back to bed herself. She awoke at four, though Max didn't, and got up to stare into his crib in disbelief. He was sound asleep.

At five she woke again to silence. A glance into Max's crib showed him still fast asleep.

When she woke again, sunlight streamed through the window and made warm patterns on the bed. It was after eight o'clock.

Dori bounded out of bed and found the crib empty. She felt a moment's panic, until she became aware of the aroma of fresh-brewed coffee and...something else.

She padded halfway down the stairs in her shirt. "Sal?" she shouted.

"Yeah?" he shouted back.

"You have Max?"

"Yeah. He's eating Cheerios."

She frowned on the shadowy stairway. "I don't have Cheerios."

"I found a box in the back of a cupboard," he answered. "It's full of flour, oats. You know, the kinds of things you cook with. You probably never even looked in it."

She accepted that taunt with a "Cute, Dominguez!"

"There's a sausage omelette waiting for you, and a croissant," he cajoled.

That sounded promising. Fattening, but promising.

"I'll be right there!" She ran back upstairs, found a blue-and-white checked cotton robe among Harper's things, and carried yesterday's clothes down with her to put them in the laundry later.

Max sat in a high chair, Cheerios all over his tray.

He laughed as Dori approached, kicking excitedly and moving the little circles of cereal around with the sweep of a tiny hand.

She leaned over him to kiss his cheek. "Hey, big guy," she said, helping herself to a Cheerio. "I didn't even hear you get up."

"I was up early, checking the cupboards and making a grocery list," Sal said. He folded an omelette in a small frying pan, then took the pan off the burner and angled it to cook the still-liquid part of the egg. "I heard him talking to himself and went up to investigate." He flipped the omelette onto a plate, added two pieces of toast and handed it to her. "When I saw that you were still asleep, I brought him down with me."

"Thank you," she said, putting her plate on the table, then pouring coffee into the two cups he'd set out. "But I was kidding about the personal servant remark last night." She replaced the pot and took her chair.

He retrieved his own plate from the oven and brought it to the table, then sat opposite her. Max's high chair was pulled up at a right-angle to their chairs.

"You sure?" he asked, handing her a jar of apricot jam. She took a bite of the omelette. It contained broccoli and cheese, and was delicious. "Well, maybe if you'd consider being a kitchen servant."

"Sure. But the galley's going to need a few supplies. Want to go shopping first thing, then I'll watch Max and get things organized in here while you work on your book?"

"I need something from the library." She spread jam on a piece of toast and put the jar within his reach. "Why don't I go there and meet you at the market? I'll take Max with me."

Sal shook his head. "I don't want you and Max alone."

"It's just a block..." she began to argue.

He shook his head. "Sorry. It's a principle of guarding someone. You never leave them alone."

She sighed. "You mean we're going to have to spend every waking moment together?"

"Not together," he placated, "but in the same place at the same time."

"We're going to get awfully tired of each other," she warned. She wasn't entirely sure that was true. He did look rather fascinating this morning in black cotton slacks and a black T-shirt.

"That'll help us remember our deal," he said, picking a wayward Cheerio off the table and putting it on Max's tray.

Her conscience pricked her, and she took offense. "Is that a reference to my kissing you while I was dreaming?" she asked coolly.

"No," he replied with a quick smile across the table. "It was a reference to my response when you kissed me."

That deflated her sense of indignation. He'd turned it all around on her. She felt like a woman in a spin—disoriented, confused.

Good work, Dominguez, Sal praised himself silently, happy with the uncertain look in Dori's eyes. Considering what she'd put him through since he'd known her, and the past two years particularly, he liked knowing she was feeling off balance.

She dropped the conversation to concentrate on her breakfast, then washed Max's hands and face and took him into the downstairs bedroom to get him ready for the trip to town.

Sal cleaned up the kitchen, then waited for her in the living room.

The house had a comfortable beachy feel that he remembered from his brief visit three years ago. There were hideous antiques all over—a clock set in a horse collar, and a lamp with ruffles too ugly to describe.

But there were also lovely country crafts the McKeon women had made—a curtain of ribbon and shells in the kitchen, a window frame decorated with moss and dried flowers. These, along with the toys and baby things scattered around the house, all conspired to create a welcoming coziness.

"We're ready," Dori said, coming out of the room in stone-colored shorts and a dark blue shirt. Max, in her arms, wore yellow overalls and a white-and-yellow striped shirt. She pinched Max's cheek. "Isn't this the cutest baby you've ever seen?"

Dancer's Beach was a carefully preserved example

of small-town America, Sal thought, as Dori pulled into a parking spot in front of Coast Groceries. Up and down the street, postwar storefronts with large plate-glass windows were interspersed with late-nineteenth century buildings with wood trim and small-paned windows.

There was an old hotel, the Buckley Arms, named after the founding family of Dancer's Beach, three brothers who ran a mill on a knoll overlooking the ocean. A ship carrying dancers from San Francisco, heading for the mining camps in the Klondike, ran aground off the coast. The brothers rescued four of the women, who gave the town its name.

A small, picturesque church with a spire stood in the middle of everything and opposite a park bordered by a library and a playground. City Hall stood just beyond it. Sal remembered with a pang that he and Dori had met several times in that park to talk about Julie. Beyond the park was an Italianate building that housed a theater and office space.

There were hanging baskets of flowers, larger than he remembered them, and park benches in the middle of every block for sitting and soaking up the charm of the small coastal town.

While in Seattle with its traffic, congestion and hurried pace, he'd dreamed of this place with its intimate little downtown and its sense of neighborly cooperation.

"First thing I have to do," Dori said, interrupting his personal analysis of Dancer's Beach, "is buy one of those strollers where the seat comes off to be a carrier."

He took Max from her as she hauled him out of the back. "I didn't know there was such a thing."

She pointed up the street. "There's a shop called Baby, Baby! that has everything. I'm sure my family won't mind my using the crib and the high chair, since they're always passing such things around, but the strollers always go home with them." Then, noticing unusual activity as merchants began to pull tables and racks out onto the sidewalk, she smiled delightedly. "Sal, there's a sidewalk sale today."

"Do we need a sidewalk?" he asked gravely.

She gave him a look of mock disgust, her eyes alight with amusement. "That joke is so old, it probably came over on the ship with the dancers!"

"And I thought I was being clever. It looks like an old Mexican marketplace."

"Come on. Let's see if Baby, Baby! has anything on sale!"

"Remember, that the eleven-thousand dollars doesn't belong to you," he said quietly as he followed with the baby. "I seem to recall your overspending considerably when I took you to Mexico City to shop for the wedding." She made her way around several other shoppers who apparently weren't moving fast enough. "Don't be silly," she said, with a smiling glance over her shoulder. "That's only because you'd driven me all that way. I felt obligated to buy."

Dori found the stroller-carrier combination she wanted right away. It had a dark blue pattern with cheery-faced suns, moons and stars, and it was twenty-five-percent off. She was beside herself with excitement. "Now I can buy him some clothes!"

In a section devoted to tiny designer garments, she bought several rompers, shirts, footed sleepers—because Max had a tendency to throw off his covers—and more socks. She also couldn't resist a little white cotton hat with a soft brim decorated with embroidered animals.

Sal put Max in the stroller, and Dori put the hat on him.

They waited for a reaction. But Max simply lay back, studied the new pattern above his head, and waited patiently for whatever would happen next.

"I thought babies always ripped their hats off," Sal observed, as Dori pushed the stroller.

"He obviously has more fashion sense than other babies. A white hat in the summer is the sign of a gentleman."

"Really. Even with bears and tigers on it?"

"Especially with bears and tigers on it."

"Life is full of mysteries."

Sal thanked the fates that had made him a patient man. Well, perhaps not patient precisely, but tolerant. While Max dozed, Dori stopped at every table and rack on Dancer Avenue.

She looked everything over, compared one item against another at a different shop, then finally made a decision, occasionally to change her mind and decide against it altogether.

Fighting boredom, Sal bought an Americano at the coffee bar on the bottom floor of the hotel.

"But I don't want coffee," Dori objected.

"I know," he replied, pointing the clerk to a piece of chocolate in the shape of a mouse with a licorice tail. "But if I have to follow you around, I have to have something to keep me awake. And I'm not leaving you alone. So put your shopping frenzy on pause for just a moment."

Accepting that mild reprimand, she laughed lightly and punched his arm. "There are purses on sale across the street, and I'm standing in line for coffee!"

"It's not coffee," he corrected, accepting the confection the clerk handed him and giving it to her. "It's espresso. A double shot."

"Yum! Thank you, Sal," she said, admiring the beautifully crafted little mouse. Then she heartlessly bit his head off.

Sal pretended horrified disapproval. "You murderess!" he accused, as she chewed with relish.

The clerk handed him his drink.

Dori shrugged. "It was that or pull off his tail, and that seemed cruel. This way, he never knew what hit him. *Now* can we shop for purses?"

"Lead the way," he said, taking a sip of his drink through the lid's narrow slit. "I'll be right behind you."

Purse shopping took an hour, though there were only thirty-one purses on the rack. He'd had time to count. And many of them were the same style, but in different colors.

She finally stood back and stared dispiritedly at the rack.

He pointed to the one she'd studied the longest. "What's wrong with that one?" It was a simple, square style with a front pocket and many separations inside.

"No pocket for my keys," she said.

"Your keys can't go into one of the twenty-two pockets inside?"

She made a face at him. "There are only five pockets inside, and no, they can't. I like a small pocket on the outside. They have to be accessible in the dark, or when my arms are full. Like when I'm carrying the baby."

"If it'll help you decide," he bargained, "I promise to always carry the baby."

She made another face. "What about when you're not here?"

"I told you, I won't leave you alone."

"I mean, when this is over," she clarified, "and you go back to Seattle."

She said it quickly, noting nothing significant in it until she heard the words lingering in the air. Then she looked for a moment as though she didn't know what to do. She seemed flustered, upset.

She took that purse in a dark blue and paid the clerk. "Darrick's always telling me I should have my keys in my hand when I step out of the car, anyway." She spoke cheerfully and pushed the stroller toward a stationery store.

Sal wandered after her, pleased at visible proof that she didn't like the idea of their eventual separation any more than he did.

After leaving the stationery store, they had started for the car, when Sal saw something that made him stop in his tracks. It was a hammock—an Adirondack hammock on a stand so that it didn't have to be tied to trees or poles.

The McKeons had had a hammock in the backyard when he'd visited after the Julie incident. He'd noticed when he and Max had taken a stroll through the garden before breakfast it was still there, but that it must have been left out all winter; it was mildewed and rotted in places, and looked as though it would split under a child's weight.

Sal had precious memories of a hammock in his childhood. There'd been one strung between two jacaranda trees at his grandmother's in Mazatlan. He'd liked it there, but his mother's mother hadn't liked his father, so they seldom visited. When they did, he spent time in the hammock every morning watching the birds and the clouds; then every night, watching the stars appear, searching for the constellations.

Then his mother had died, and life had changed dramatically. His father had joined his uncle and some friends to form the Cat Pack, and Sal and Julie had learned to steal.

Sal caught Dori's arm and pulled her toward the sporting goods store and the camping display.

"Oh, Sal, I'm not much of a camper," she said, frowning dubiously at the camp stove and the dried food display. "I can't cook indoors, much less over an open fire. I mean, if—"

"*Querida,*" he said, putting a silencing finger to her lips. "You do not have to go camping. And, anyway, this is for me."

"What?"

He pointed to the hammock.

"We have a hammock in the backyard," she said.

He walked around the one on display. "Have you looked at it lately?"

"Oh, yeah." She nodded. "Dillon and Harper were the last ones there before winter. They were supposed to bring it in, but Dillon and the Northwest Medical Team got called to some disaster, and they ended up leaving in a hurry."

Sal bought the hammock.

Dori smiled blandly. "It's neat, but how are we going to get it home?"

"Do you have rope in the car?"

She folded her arms. "Of course not. I don't go to many lynchings."

He rolled his eyes at her. "To tie the stand to the top of the car."

"Ah." She'd been teasing him, but he'd been so wrapped up in his memories, he'd missed it. It was unlike him not to catch a joke. "Certainly these guys must have rope."

She rummaged through a bin and emerged with a thick loop of bright yellow cord. "Will this do?"

"Beautifully. Do you have a tarp or a blanket in the trunk?"

She shook her head.

"What would you do if you were ever stranded?" he asked, looking through a stack of tarps leaning up against the side of a table.

She blinked at him. "How would a rope and tarp help me?" she asked. "I could shinny down a cliff, then spread the tarp in case I wanted to paint something?"

She was being smart, as she often was, and there

was something exasperating and somehow endearing about it. He took her chin in the *V* of his thumb and forefinger, and pinched gently. "The rope would have a hundred uses, and the tarp would keep you warm and dry at night."

"But, so would the car."

"What if the car was no longer habitable because of a crash or a fire, or you'd simply left it to explore and gotten lost?"

She patted her purse. "I always have my purse with me. I'd call for help on my cell phone."

"One of your brothers, no doubt."

"Probably."

"I thought you resented their interference in your life?"

"Well...saving me from death isn't really interference, is it? It's rescue. Unless you think I could fashion a rope and a tarp into a car or a magic tarp or something, and drive or fly back to civilization."

He dropped his hand from her and sighed. Explaining danger to a woman accustomed to being protected was hopeless.

"If I hadn't forced you into a decision about the purse," he reminded pointedly, "you wouldn't have had it to put the cell phone in to call your brothers."

"That's reaching, Sal," she said with a giggle.

He didn't know why he wanted to kiss her.

He bought the tarp.

"So, what did you want it for?" she asked. "Are you going to leave me stranded somewhere?"

"No," he said, scolding her with a look. "I wanted

to protect the roof of your car from the hammock stand."

She patted his shoulder. "Well, that's very considerate. Once you get it attached to the roof, I'll take you to lunch."

It was simply done, Max offering encouragement from the stroller.

Dori stood back to admire the tarp-wrapped stand securely fastened through the open windows. "Ah…" she said. "How do we get back in the car? The doors are tied closed."

"I put you in through the window," he explained, "then hand you the baby."

Her eyes went up and down his long body. He felt as though she'd touched him from head to toe.

"Can *you* get in through the window?"

"You forget what I used to do for a living," he said with a grin. "I can get through any window."

She studied him for a moment, then arched an eyebrow. "Maybe I'll make one of my characters a jewel thief," she speculated. "Maybe even the hero." Her eyes lost focus as she considered the idea. Then they fixed on him again, bright with excitement.

"I wonder if a reader today would consider a thief-hero sympathetic?" she asked, unconsciously hooking her arm in his. They'd stowed the stroller frame, and he carried Max in the carrier. "I mean, would they love him, anyway, even if he steals?"

"I suppose it depends on why he steals."

"True. If I made his motivation something noble. Like yours was."

He was happy to know she thought that.

"But he'd have to reform in the end."

"Of course."

"But..." She still sounded troubled. "Would a reader love him?"

"You did," he reminded her.

CHAPTER FIVE

DORI WAS CHATTY and cheerful through lunch, feeding Max tiny bites of cottage cheese with one hand while picking at her fruit salad with the other.

She kept up a stream of conversation about their purchases, thoughts about her book, questions about Sal's business. Inside she was wondering why she felt stricken at the thought of his return to Seattle.

She was still angry with Sal, still resentful that he'd left her at the altar after their wedding; hurt, now that she thought about it, that he hadn't made more of an effort in the past two years even to talk to her about what had happened. But this strange situation with the baby and the money was forcing her to be civil and to cooperate with him until they solved the mystery.

That was all that was confusing her, she thought with some relief. When a woman was angry, she should be able to behave angrily, not be forced to pretend everything was fine. That was unnatural and bound to blur what she really felt—even in her own mind.

Feeling better now that she'd reasoned that out, Dori pushed the cart in Coast Groceries, while they talked over meal possibilities and Sal tossed food into the cart.

Car loaded with food, they headed home, where Sal set up the collapsible playpen, then sent her upstairs to write.

Dori made every effort to clear her mind of all her concerns and concentrate on the book. This was what was going to set the direction of the rest of her life, she told herself as she spread out her notes on the scholarly work she'd intended to write and restructured them to form a novel.

She had to accept that the process would set her back three weeks, but now that she had a child to support, she had to give thought to the book's marketability rather than simply her own sense of accomplishment in producing it.

She had to call Athena Hartford, she told herself, making a note on a Post-it that she attached to the shade of her lamp.

It was almost six o'clock when Sal called her to dinner. The sun remained high and bright, and they ate outside at a picnic table under an old ash tree. Max, already fed, played with a rattle in the playpen.

Sal had made taco salads, a favorite of hers, with the added touch of a large Anaheim pepper stuffed with cheese, then rolled in eggs and cracker crumbs and fried.

"It's wonderful," she said simply. "You must have girlfriends all over the place who adore you for your cooking."

"Of course I don't," he said, holding up his left hand with the ring she'd put there. "I'm a married man. How'd your afternoon go?"

"Good," she said, ignoring that remark. "I have

enough of the plot in mind to be able to convert some of what I've already done to background and also use it to give substance to my heroine's work. I've just gotten started, of course, but I've written a couple of pages and I'm excited about it."

"I'm sure that'll help carry you through." He pointed across the lawn to where the hammock was set up in a pool of sunlight. "Max and I mowed the lawn and assembled the hammock before we made dinner."

"Have you tested it yet?"

He shook his head. "I thought I'd do that after dinner. You are going to reward me by doing the dishes?"

"Of course."

"Good. Then I don't have to withhold the flan I made for dessert."

She paused, a forkful of flavorful beef, cheese and lettuce halfway to her mouth. "You didn't!"

"I did. Couldn't find Mexican vanilla, but it should be palatable all the same."

"You are a treasure."

"I know," he said modestly.

"In the kitchen, anyway."

He gave her a quick, suggestive look as he took a sip of wine. "I'm a treasure in a lot of places," he said, "but you didn't hang around to find out."

She was determined to maintain peace. "Let's not talk about that," she said, putting the bite in her mouth.

"We have to sometime," he persisted.

She shook her head as she chewed and swallowed.

"No, we don't. It doesn't matter now. If we intended to stay together, maybe we'd have to straighten it out. But since we don't, it doesn't make any difference."

He shook his head. "That's your usual illogical assessment of things," he said, his words sharp but his tone mild. "It's the *reason* you left. Don't you think your attitude might change if you really understood what happened?"

"No," she replied candidly. "I know all I need to know. And let's not pollute this wonderful dinner with discussions of the past. It's over."

"Maybe for you," he said quietly.

"Take the ring off," she advised. "Let it be over for you, too."

He took another sip of wine, a long one. "I'm not running away. I made promises, took vows."

"That you ignored two minutes after the ceremony was finished!" She slammed a fist on the table. Crockery shook, and Max looked up in alarm.

"But you don't want to know why?" Sal asked.

"No." She swung her legs out from under the table and began to gather up dishes. "I remember how much it hurt. I don't want to hear you validate that with some charming explanation that still won't justify the past two years."

She marched into the kitchen.

When she went back outside with a tray to carry in the leftover food and the dishes, Sal and Max were lying in the hammock. The baby was on Sal's chest, Sal's brimmed hat protecting Max from the sun. Max was babbling, and Sal replied as though he understood what the baby was saying.

'I am never speaking to him again,' Dori told herself as she covered the salad bowl with cling wrap and put it in the refrigerator. She spotted six clear glass cups of flan and took one. With the can of whipped cream from the shelf in the door, she created a tall column of topping and stood at the counter to enjoy the dessert. She was aware of the wonderful taste and texture, but her mood made her unable to enjoy it.

She cleaned up the kitchen, started the dishwasher, and went back outside to bring in the tablecloth. Max was banging on Sal's face and squealing with delight.

Men, Dori thought in disgust, and went to put some things in the washer. Then she headed for Sal's room, tiptoeing as though he might hear her from outside, and took a change of clothes and underwear for herself and Max for tomorrow.

Maybe one of those bars that fit over the top of the door with a clothes hanger attached would simplify her life. Then she could have a few changes of clothes in her room upstairs.

Looking for underwear, she opened the drawer in which she usually kept it, only to find it filled with briefs and T-shirts. She stared at them in surprise.

"I've heard of panty raids," a lazy male voice said from behind her, "but never a briefs raid."

She turned to find him standing just inside the room, Max on his hip, a pudgy arm hooked around Sal's. They were quite a picture, handsome man and beautiful child, dark features and Latino good looks making them appear related.

Mine, she thought in a moment of painful longing. *That's what I could have had if he hadn't left me.*

She knew that thought to be counterproductive, and pushed it away. "I was looking for my own underwear," she said. "Did you move it?"

"Next drawer down," he said, coming to pull it open and show her. "This is the only drawer I've taken."

"It's all right." She quickly snatched two pairs of panties, a bra and a couple of pairs of socks. She scooped up the clothes she'd dropped on the bed. "I'll take these upstairs," she said politely, determined to put their personal issues aside, "then I'll watch Max while you relax."

"I have a few phone calls to make, but that's about all."

"I'll be right down."

When Dori returned, Sal took the cordless phone into the kitchen while she spread a blanket on the floor for Max, then found a sitcom on television.

One eye on the TV and the other on the baby, Dori sat on the edge of the blanket and leaned against the bottom of the sofa. Max turned and rolled and "swam" his way across the blanket. Dori turned him around, and he eventually worked his way back. He inspected one toy after another, dropped them and picked them up, and occasionally threw them at Dori.

Sal returned, phone in hand. He placed it on the coffee table a few feet away from her. "Want some popcorn?" he asked. "Or coffee and flan?"

She met his eyes, refusing to look guilty. "I've already had my flan, thank you. I'm sorry I didn't wait for you, but I wasn't speaking to you at the time. So I ate it all by myself.''

He laughed. "No need to explain. Also no need to feel limited to one. You want another?"

It was an agonizing decision. While she was making it, the phone rang.

As though in slow motion, she saw Sal reach for the cordless, and realized what she would be put through if that was her mother on the line.

She leapt across the edge of blanket and grabbed all she could reach of Sal—his pants leg. "No!" she shrieked, reaching for the phone with her free hand. "No, don't answer it!"

He looked down in amused disbelief at her hand clutching the fabric of his pants just above the knee. "Why not?"

"It could be my mother!"

He looked down at the readout and read the number aloud.

"That's her!" Dori whispered harshly. "Give it to me!"

He held it out of reach. "Why?"

She tugged on the material she held, as the phone continued to ring. "Because if she hears your voice, *I'll* never hear the end of it! She'll be ordering wedding invitations and hiring a hall!"

"But she's too late for that."

"She doesn't know that. Sal, give me the phone!"

"Deception," he said didactically, "is its own trap."

"Don't preach to me!" she snarled. "Just give me the phone!"

He finally handed it to her.

"And don't say a word while I'm on the line!" she ordered in a loud whisper, then pushed the talk button. "Hi, Mom," she said pleasantly, still glowering at Sal. "How's Dad doing?"

With an indulgent shake of his head, Sal went into the kitchen.

"Oh, you know your father," her mother said with acceptance. "He can't dance the jig, so he's discouraged. The doctor told him it'll take time, that he has to do his exercises—but all he does is complain and watch ESPN. I thought maybe you could talk to him."

Peg McKeon was in her early sixties, a short, round woman with a charming but bossy disposition, and a particularly aggressive approach to Dori's love life.

Charlie McKeon, on the other hand, was laid-back and sweet, and Dori missed his sudden appearances on her doorstep with care packages from her mother. He was tall and barrel-chested, and had had bad knees since Dori entered college. When they finally prevented him from getting on the floor with his grandchildren, he decided to do something about it.

"Put him on," Dori said to her mother.

"Hey, sweetheart," his gruff, strong voice said.

"Don't 'sweetheart' me," Dori scolded firmly. "I want to know why you aren't doing your exercises."

"Because they hurt," he replied. "I do them, just not as many as I'm supposed to."

"And that's probably why you're not recovering as quickly as you want to."

"I'm slow recovering," he said with significant

emphasis, "because I'm being nursed by Nagging Nellie! 'Do this. Don't eat that. Walk around. Don't sit there. Are you watching that again?'"

"She's just trying to take care of you, Daddy," Dori placated, secretly grateful she wasn't the one confined with her mother. "She wants you to get better. And if you don't promise me you'll do *all* your exercises, I'll call Dillon."

"He's still in Europe," her father said with a sigh. "Or I'm sure your mother would have him here. Why she had to call you today, I'll never know."

Dori laughed. "You know Mom. She's not happy unless she has the entire family turned against the evildoer, whichever one of us that is at the time. That's what she thinks family is for—not to support you, but to gang up against you."

He laughed. "You've got that right."

"But I mean it," Dori said, firming her voice. "You do what you're told, or I'll come over there myself and cook for you."

"Now, there's no call to get mean," he admonished. "Peg, she's threatening to come and cook for us."

"Well, promise her you'll be good," Dori heard her mother say in the background. "There's no reason I should suffer, too."

"Bye, baby," her father said.

"Bye, Daddy," she replied. "I don't want to hear any more bad reports on you."

There was a rustling on the other end of the line as the phone changed hands. "Dori," her mother said.

"It would be lovely to have you visit. And you don't have to cook. Really."

"I will, Mom," she promised. "Maybe in a week or two. I'm doing really well on the book, and I hate to lose momentum."

"That's wonderful," Peg praised. "Are you remembering to eat?"

Remembering to eat. She'd eaten more today than she usually ate in a week. "I am," she replied.

"Are you sleeping well?"

That was a hilarious question, considering Max's presence in her life. But her mother didn't know about him, and Dori had to keep it that way if she didn't want instant and major interference.

"I'm doing fine," she insisted. "Coming here was a great—" Before Dori could finish the thought, Max, trapped against the sofa and unable to move, shouted his need for assistance.

"What was that?" Peg asked.

Dori picked him up, turned him around and set him down again.

"What was what?"

"That squeal. Like a baby."

There was no use denying what her mother had heard. "I'm baby-sitting for the neighbors," she said.

"The Fishers?" her mother asked. "They're our age."

Dori knew the Fishers. They were on a cruise at the moment, but her mother didn't necessarily know that. And Dori knew they had a daughter who had a young baby.

"Their daughter's visiting with her baby," she

said. "They were going to a movie, and I was just going to hang around and watch television, so..."

"As good as you are with babies," Peg interrupted, "you should have your own, you know."

"Mom, don't start," Dori pleaded.

"I'm not starting, but neither are you. You should think about that. You're getting up there, you know."

"Twenty-six isn't 'up there.'"

"It isn't eighteen."

"Mom."

"Well."

Dori recognized that tone of voice. Her mother was giving up, but not without audible signs that she was the misunderstood and mistreated victim of the conversation.

"When you feel inclined to visit, we'll be here."

"I'll call first."

"We'll be waiting."

Dori turned off the phone, exhausted.

"Why didn't you tell her about the baby?" Sal asked, handing her a bowl of popcorn. "Yes, I was eavesdropping."

"When I tell her," Dori replied, "she'll be here like a shot, Dad on crutches or not, and I don't want that to happen while *you're* here. She'll think it means there's something going on between us again."

"And you're afraid she'll find out we're married." He put a can of cola down beside her popcorn. "Why didn't you ever tell your family?"

"You know why," she said, reaching for the baby as he hoisted himself toward her leg. She stood him on his feet on her thighs and smiled into his bright-eyed little face. "It'll be just one more thing that proves to them how incapable I am of managing my life, or attracting a man, or carrying through with anything but education."

He looked confused as he went to the kitchen for his popcorn and coke. When he returned, he sat beside her. He took the clicker off the coffee table and muted the sound on the television.

"I don't understand," he said. "Isn't marriage proof that you *were* able to attract a man?"

"When he left me immediately after the ceremony? I don't think so."

"Ah." He took a sip of his drink and put the glass on a coaster on the coffee table. "I hadn't thought that through. You did turn our marriage into something you didn't have to finish."

"You," she said pointedly, "turned it into something I *couldn't* finish. And why didn't you tell them?"

"To help you out. I could tell you hadn't."

"Since you'd ruined my life, that was very considerate of you."

He groaned. "Let's not go through that again. The point is, someday she will have to know about the wedding, and you won't be able to hide the baby forever."

"I don't intend to. Just for the time being. Put the sound back on, please—this story was just getting interesting."

A COUPLE ON TELEVISION were kissing. Sal would have preferred to watch baseball or the news or anything other than a man and a woman locked in a passionate embrace. Living in close proximity with Dori was taking its toll on him.

He thought about making love to her all the time. When he'd gone to Desi's rescue, when he'd put himself between her and Paco and taken a bullet in the shoulder, and the police had hauled him away and he'd been driven to the hospital in an ambulance that hit every pothole, he'd been sustained by the knowledge that when he got home, he would make love to Dori at last.

And instead, he'd found her gone. The bullet wound had been a nuisance compared to the ache in his heart.

But he sat without complaint, telling himself that if he just stayed with it and did his best to see this through, he'd find his moment. She'd loved him once; he could make her love him again. But she wasn't a woman one could push or force. She had to come to him in her own time.

All he had to do was remain sane that long.

The love scene over, she lifted Max up and down. He giggled happily, catching a fistful of her bangs and pulling.

"Ah! Sal!" she pleaded.

Sal put his popcorn aside and turned to free her hair from the baby's fingers. It was as silky to the touch as he remembered, but he wasn't wild about the new style.

"Thank you," she said, turning Max around so that he faced the television while she bounced him. He seemed pleased with the new distraction.

"Why did you cut your hair?" Sal asked.

"It was part of the new me. It helped me change direction." She put a hand to it with a side-glance of self-deprecation. "You should have seen it at first. It was a buzzcut. About half an inch all around."

"Aerodynamic, at least," he said.

She laughed. "Yes. It cut my morning getting-ready ritual in half."

"And why did you need a new direction?"

"After dreaming about…" she began, then apparently changed her mind. "I decided it was time I went to work on the book instead of just talking about it. And that seemed to require that I streamline everything. Even my hair."

"Did you like teaching?"

"Sometimes. The kids were great, but there's a lot of politics going on in a school, a lot of things taking place behind the scenes that I'm not crazy about. But I may have to learn to live with it, with a child to support." She turned to him, her eyes lively with interest. "What about you? Are you enjoying the security business?"

"Yes, mostly. Every once in a while there's a client I'd be happy to abandon to whoever's after him, but I try to remember that I don't have to like everyone."

"Your secretary's very pretty."

She made that observation while pretending to peer around the bouncing baby at the television, as though his reply didn't matter. Did he detect jealousy?

"Yes, she is," he replied simply.

"She seems to like babies."

"She has three of her own."

She turned to him. "Really."

He nodded. "All girls."

"So she's married."

"Widowed."

"Oh."

She said it casually, but he heard the subtle sound of disappointment. "He was a cop. Died in a car wreck while in pursuit of a robbery suspect, just before she came to work for us."

"Poor thing."

"She seems to be coping well. She looks like a fashion model without a care in the world, but she's really all soul and substance."

Max started to fuss, and she turned him around and put him on her shoulder. "I think he's winding down. Time for his bottle."

Sal put a hand to her shoulder when she tried to get to her knees to stand.

"I'll get it for you. Do you want to sit with him in the rocking chair in my bedroom?"

"You don't mind?"

"Of course not." He took Max from her and helped her up. He handed the baby back, then went to the refrigerator for a bottle, while she went into his room.

He ran the bottle under hot water and tried not to think about her sitting just a few feet away from his bed.

He took the bottle in to her and saw that Max already had his head on her shoulder, eyes glazed with weariness. But the baby straightened at the sight of the bottle. When she repositioned him he lay back eagerly and put both hands up to help hold it.

"One more thing, please?" she asked.

"Yes?"

"His blanket. I think it's still in the playpen in the kitchen."

Sal retrieved it and tucked it between the baby and Dori's arm. His fingertips brushed the tip of her breast, startling both of them. For an instant, he didn't move, and she stopped the rocking that would have taken them out of contact.

They looked into each other's eyes, remembering, imagining.

Then he remembered his decision to be subtle and cool, and asked, as though nothing had happened, "Anything else?"

"Nothing, thanks," she replied in the same even tone.

He left the room and went to turn the television to a news channel.

She emerged about ten minutes later and carried a sleeping Max upstairs. She was back down in a few minutes and went to open the front door.

"Paper's here," she said, bending down to retrieve a thin newspaper rolled up tightly and secured with a rubber band. "It's just a weekly, but it's full of local news and gossip. The new television schedule for the week is in it tonight."

She closed and locked the door, slipped off the rubber band and unrolled the paper as she walked toward the sofa. She stopped halfway into the room and gasped. "Sal!" she exclaimed.

"What?"

She peered at him around the side of the newspaper. "I think I've just solved the mystery of Max's money." She walked toward him and sat cross-legged on the floor beside him. "You won't believe this," she said, reading an article on the front page.

He muted the television. "Believe what?"

"Faith Community Church had an auction to raise money for their new roof."

"Yes?"

"The Sunday School Mothers got donations from all the merchants in town."

"Yes?"

"Burgers by the Sea catered a prime rib dinner at cost."

"Generous."

"The choir entertained during dinner with a medley of pop tunes from—"

"Dori! The point?"

She sat down beside him and put the paper on his lap. "'Pastor Price took the evening's earnings home with him to the parsonage,'" she read aloud, "'and, lacking a safe in which to protect the cash overnight, locked it in the drawer of the desk in his office. When he went into his office the following morning after breakfast, he found that the lock had been broken and the drawer stood open—empty.'"

She pointed to the last paragraph of the story.

"'The auction's take,'" she read, "'was $11,572.'"

CHAPTER SIX

"WE KNOW who to return the money to!" Dori said excitedly to Sal. "I'll do it first thing in the morning."

He shook his head. "I don't think so."

She huffed with impatience. "Why not?"

"Just a hunch," he said. "I don't think that Max's mother is the one who stole the money in the first place."

Dori nodded. "I know, I know. You think it's her boyfriend, or pimp, or whatever. But what difference does that make to returning the money?"

"If you return the money, there'll be press coverage," he said. "Or, even if there wasn't, this is a small town. Someone will remember you walking into the parsonage."

"So?"

"I'll bet they'll conclude that if you had the money, you also have the baby. Right now, they don't know who has either. When you and I are out with Max together, we're just another family and nobody notices, but once everyone knows you had the money…"

He was right. But she didn't like it.

"So the poor church has to go without a roof?"

Sal shook his head. "I'll have Diego make an anonymous donation right into the church account."

She brightened. "You'd do that?"

"First thing in the morning."

She studied him for a moment, remembering the kind but tough and unyielding man he'd been during the Julie incident.

"You were always a sensitive man," she said, noticing for the first time a subtle change around his eyes and in the line of his mouth. "But I don't remember this sweetness in you before. And I don't understand how you've managed to acquire it while operating a security company."

He put a hand to his eyes as though trying to hide. "Dori, I don't think it's acceptable to tell a bodyguard you consider him 'sweet.' I'm sure there's a law against it somewhere. In fact, the law enforcement world calls us 'hard men.'"

She was amused by his embarrassment. "Well, you don't define yourself by your work, do you? You're also a man who helped a criminal reform so that he could be a grandfather to his daughter's babies.... You were so efficient and innovative in supervising the addition to and renovation of a hospital that your plans are now a model for similar constructions funded by charity.... Max thinks you're wonderful...."

It occurred to her that she might have gone a little over the top there. She understood why he didn't want her to return the money, but the idea that he would anonymously restore the cash himself, so the church wouldn't suffer while he kept her safe made her completely forget the animosity between them.

He smiled. "One wonders then, why *you* have no use for me."

She began to wonder herself, but she wasn't willing to admit it. So she fell back on the old argument.

"The last time I had use for you, you weren't there."

"And there's no forgiving that?" he asked quietly. "Ever?"

Saying no would make her sound selfish and heartless and open a whole area of discussion she couldn't even think about at this hour. And so would saying yes.

"I have to go," she said instead, avoiding his eyes, knowing she was being cowardly as she backed toward the kitchen and the stairs. "Next time we go to town, I have to get a baby monitor so that I can hear him and know what's going on."

His eyes told her he knew precisely what she was doing. "Hmm," he said. "I wonder if they'd have a Dori monitor to help me know what's going on with you?"

She turned and headed for the stairs. "Good night," she called.

"Yeah," he replied.

THEY HAD CEREAL, fruit and yogurt for breakfast, and steered clear of all contentious topics of discussion.

"You're sure there isn't something *you* want to do this morning?" Dori asked Sal, as she fed Max baby cereal and bananas. Fortunately, Max was hungry and used only a few spoonfuls to decorate the room.

Sal shook his head. "I'm going to call Diego, but I can do that while Max and I are getting some sun."

"I feel guilty," she confessed.

"Good," he replied, clearing the table. "I'll have a chip to use in my favor one day. Are you wide awake enough to work? I heard you get up with him a couple of times."

"I think so. He went right back to sleep twice, so I managed almost five hours."

He handed her a thermos. "Made you some tea. And if you tell me that's sweet, I'll get very upset."

She laughed. "Can I say it's thoughtful?"

"Thoughtful's acceptable. And if you'd like to reward me for it in any way…" He let the suggestion trail off, his expression blandly innocent.

But she knew what he had in mind. And the very thought of kissing him made the blood rush to her cheeks. It was a stupid schoolgirl reaction that she couldn't stop because a kiss suggested intimacy, and two years ago they'd both eagerly anticipated an intimacy that had never happened. An intimacy that was now probably on his mind as much as it was on hers.

She saw him note her blush as she stood and pushed her chair in. "I could make you a character in my book," she said, pretending to be unaware of her own reaction and his surprise at it. She held up her cup. "I'll take this with me for the tea."

"Good idea," he said, apparently willing to let the moment pass. Proving that he could be thoughtful *and* sweet.

Feeling as though the world was a very confusing place, Dori wiped off the baby's face and kissed his cheek. Then she hurried upstairs to spend the morning with the fictional people she was beginning to understand more than real people.

She went downstairs for a snack and to stretch her legs at a quarter to eleven, bringing the already empty thermos with her. In the quiet kitchen she filled the kettle and put it on to boil. Then she looked out the window to see Sal, the baby on his hip and the cell phone to his ear, pacing the backyard.

She felt herself smile. She was amazed and frankly touched by how easily he'd taken to the baby. She would miss him when it was time for them to go their separate ways.

She could forgive him for having left her on their wedding day to run to Desi's aid, she realized now, but she could never love him again with the wholehearted devotion she'd felt at that time.

The kettle having boiled, she filled the thermos, dropped in a tea bag and went back upstairs to work.

At a quarter to one, she copied her work onto a disk, expecting Sal's call to lunch. When it didn't come, she worked a little longer.

At one-fifteen, she turned off the computer and chased down a detail she needed in her source materials.

When he still hadn't called at one-thirty, she went downstairs to investigate.

She found sandwiches and fruit salads on covered plates in the refrigerator. Peering out the screen door, she saw the picnic table set and the playpen covered with a bedsheet, Max fast asleep inside. Sal was asleep in the hammock.

Dori went out into the lazy afternoon, the sun warm, insects droning, and felt herself drawn to the hammock.

It was safe, she told herself. He was asleep.

A little breeze ruffled his thick black hair, and his dark, straight eyelashes gleamed in the sunlight. His mouth and the line of his jaw were relaxed—something she never saw during the day—and his fingers were laced together over his flat stomach. He'd kicked off his tennis shoes, and his white stockinged feet were crossed at the ankles.

She couldn't count the number of times she'd dreamed of him lying beside her. Or the number of times she'd awakened in the night so sure that she had only to reach out to touch him. But the sheet beside her had been cold and empty.

And now here he was, warm and vital, even in his sleep. Longing escaped her in a gasp that hurt as it left her throat.

His eyes opened lazily, slitted against the sun. He saw her, caught her wrist and pulled her down beside him.

"No," she began to protest. "I have to..."

"Shh," he whispered, putting his fingertips to her lips as he fitted her against him.

The hammock swayed with the action. She knew she should fight this, but she'd wanted it for so long.

She flung an arm across his waist, searching for steadiness in the swaying hammock. He covered it with his own, his palm closing around her elbow.

She opened her mouth to speak, but he shushed her again. "Rest," he said softly. "The sun is very restoring. It feels like Mexico this afternoon."

Mexico. She could remember his rancho and the bed she'd dreamed of sharing. They'd have lain just like this, bodies touching...

She resisted her body's willingness to relax. This was trouble. She shouldn't...

He stroked gently up and down her upper arm. "Easy, *querida*," he said, his lips in her hair. "Be easy."

And suddenly, fighting it was just too hard, too contrary to everything she felt, everything she wanted. She let her body relax into his, curves and hollows finding their place against his hard planes.

She hiked a leg up over his, felt the sun massage her body as though it were a soothing hand, and fell asleep.

"GOOD ONE, *muchacho*," Sal told himself, as her knee brushed up his thigh and settled right where she would probably have liked to put it two years ago. The pressure was gentle and wouldn't have been painful if he hadn't wanted her so much, hadn't imagined them lying just like this—only without clothes to hamper their explorations.

In his imagination, she was awake and eager for him. But right now he'd settle for this pale imitation of his dreams.

And if he were honest with himself, it wasn't so pale at all. Loss and time had taught him that the passion he'd thought so essential to his existence two years ago was no longer as important as a softly whispered *I don't remember this sweetness in you.*

She'd found something to like in the man he was inside. And for now, that, and an armful of her even though she was fully clothed and fast asleep, would keep him going.

SAL AWOKE to a sense of being smothered. Remembering instantly that Dori had been lying in his arms when he fell asleep, he tried to assess whether she remained.

If she did, he didn't want to make a sudden move and frighten her. If she didn't, it was entirely possible that she was taking advantage of his being asleep to finally do him in, as she'd threatened when he'd left her at San Ignacio's.

He opened his eyes slowly, almost afraid of what he'd see. A pillow pressed to his face? A blanket?

It was fur. Orange fur. In July? Dori hadn't been wearing fur.

Without warning, the fur shifted. Sal drew a long, welcome breath and looked into a pair of round gold eyes—eyes with elliptical pupils. Cat's eyes.

The nature of the owner of the fur was confirmed an instant later when a scratchy tongue slurped his nose.

He put a hand up to assess the size and shape of the cat.

As though reading Sal's intention, the cat stood on his chest, straddling Dori's arm, and stretched a striped, orange body until he was up on the tips of four white feet, his white-tipped tail curling and uncurling. White-tipped ears pointed straight up, and preposterously long whiskers seemed to curl in, then roll out like party favors.

The cat settled down again, purring, looking very much as though he intended to spend the afternoon.

"Well, hello, Cat," Sal said, scratching him between the ears. The cat closed his eyes and purred more loudly.

Sal had had a cat as a child, but it had been left with a neighbor when he'd followed his father and uncle to embark upon a life of crime.

Since then, he'd been in Texas part of the time, in Mexico part of the time, and now he lived in a condo that didn't allow pets.

Dori raised her head and opened her eyes, looking disoriented and still sleepy.

She looked at the cat, then at Sal. "Who's this?" she asked.

He was pleased that her interest in the cat had forestalled any embarrassment she might have felt at waking up in his arms. "Ah...I'm not sure," he replied. "He hasn't told me."

The cat licked the underside of Dori's chin.

She smiled and stroked the cat's head. He leaned toward her and pressed his body into hers.

She giggled and looked at Sal to share the moment. She was propped on an elbow that was digging into his chest, but he wasn't about to complain.

"Well, he's a cutie." She scratched his neck. "He doesn't have a collar."

"A lot of cats don't wear one."

"True."

"He might live anywhere around here."

"But he's chosen to spend the afternoon with us. I'll get him some milk." She pushed herself up, apparently forgetting that they lay in a hammock, shifted her weight as though to stand and, before he could shout a warning, dumped the three of them onto the grass.

The cat screamed and shot away as though from a cannon, and Sal and Dori landed in a tidy pile, Sal uppermost, braced on his forearms.

"Well, this is only fair," he said, stroking her short spiky hair back from her pink and flustered-looking face. "You slept on me for about an hour."

"You...invited me," she said, sounding breathless.

"I did." It was going to take superhuman effort to let her up, and he was beginning to believe he wouldn't be able to, when there was a shriek from the playpen.

Sal rolled off Dori, and she was up like a shot, her concern for Max turning to laughter. His cry had been excitement, not alarm or distress. The orange cat looked at him through the nylon mesh of the playpen.

Dori pulled the sheet off the top of the playpen and lifted Max into her arms. Sal scooped the cat up with a hand under his belly and brought him toward the baby. Dori took Max's hand and stroked the cat's fur.

"This is a cat, Maxie," she said. "And if you treat him nicely, he'll be your friend."

Max shrieked again, and the cat, unsure of the baby's intentions, leaped down and watched him from behind Sal's legs.

"Would you get him a saucer of milk?" Dori asked

Sal. "I'll put Max back in the playpen. He might enjoy just watching the cat long enough for us to eat our sandwiches."

Max was fascinated with the cat. And, apparently, the cat was fascinated with Dori and Sal, or at least with their ability to provide milk and chicken, because he was still there when night fell. He made himself comfortable in the basil, oregano and thyme Julie had planted in the window box outside the kitchen window.

"Should I let him in?" Dori asked Sal, peering back at the cat, who looked in at her. It was an I'm-starving-and-lonely-and-have-no-one-but-you look.

Max leaned out of Sal's arms and stretched both little hands toward the cat.

"It's your house," Sal reminded her.

She made a face at him. "That's the point. It's not. It belongs to my brothers, and there's no one here a lot of the time. And I live in an apartment in Edenfield. What'll happen when I have to go home?"

He shrugged. "Maybe we'll just have to stay married so you'll have somewhere to put the cat."

He said it easily, thinking it was time he started preparing her for the fact that ultimately, that was what was going to happen.

He expected hot and instant denial, but she was apparently more worried about the cat at the moment than the future of their relationship.

"That would be no help at all," she said. "You live in a condo where you can't have animals."

Okay. He'd push this a little farther. "When we

decide to stay together," he said matter-of-factly, "we'll buy a house here."

"Really." She was beginning to catch on. She turned from the window and leaned back against the counter, folding her arms. "Where?"

"There's a great old house just up the hill behind the Bijou Theater building," he said. He'd noticed it one afternoon three years ago when he'd been exasperated with Dori and had gone for a walk. It was straight up and down, and three stories tall, set up on a bank and back from the street. It had looked freshly painted then, pale blue with dark blue trim and oyster-colored columns supporting a front porch. Children had been playing on the porch, and their laughter had caught his attention.

He described it briefly and told her how he'd found it. "I noticed yesterday when we went to town that it's for sale."

Her eyes lost focus, and he wondered if she was imagining the house filled with their children. That was probably wishful thinking on his part, but he'd been an optimist all his life.

She finally refocused on him, her expression filled with reprimand. "When you came back here with me, we made a deal."

He nodded. "Two years ago we made another deal." He raised a hand to stop her before she could reply. "Yes, I know. And I broke it." He sighed. "But that was because of another deal, and...I can't ignore that one any more than I can ignore the one you and I made."

She opened her mouth, a bitter reply on the tip of

her tongue, if he could judge by what he saw in her eyes. But she sighed and bit it back.

"We were talking about the cat," she said, deflecting a quarrel.

He couldn't believe she'd done that with all the weight of it on her side.

"I'll let it in," he said, going to the door to do just that. The cat darted in. "When the time comes to leave, we'll worry about what to do."

Smiling, she scooped the cat up into her arms and stroked him. His purr was loud and rumbling, his gratitude apparent.

"What'll we call him?" she asked. "What's orange besides marmalade. Everyone names orange cats Marmalade."

Max reached toward the cat, arms swinging excitedly. Sal wisely kept his distance.

"Uh…apricots, cheese, poppies, goldfish…"

She looked at him in exasperation. "You can't name a cat Goldfish."

"I'm trying to help," he said. "I don't hear you coming up with anything."

"Sunset?"

"Those are also pink and purple."

"Pumpkin?"

He thought about that. "That's a possibility."

"Peaches?"

He frowned his disapproval. "Please. He's a guy."

She rolled her eyes. "I know!" she said after a moment. "What about Cheddar?"

He liked that. "Cheesy," he replied, "and a little sharp, but I like it."

She shook her head at him. "I don't remember you being corny, either," she said.

"Are you beginning to wonder," he asked, "if you really knew me at all?"

She looked stricken for a moment.

Max had leaned so far out of Sal's arms trying to reach the cat that Sal had to reclaim him and settle him back on his hip amid loud protests.

"Maybe you've just changed," she observed quietly.

"Maybe," he replied. "Isn't that what time and new experiences are supposed to do to you? Make you different than you were before?"

She stared at him as though trying to decide. "I don't feel different."

He nodded grimly. "Well, maybe that's more our problem than the fact that I do." He indicated the squirming, fussy baby in his arms. "I'll get a bottle and see if I can relax him for bed. You find the cat a cozy spot."

DORI PREPARED A BOX for Cheddar, which she lined with a soft old towel from the linen closet. She placed it in a warm corner of the pantry near the water heater.

Then she picked up the cat and put him in the box. He sniffed it carefully and jumped out.

She put him back in, hoping to relay the message that it was where he belonged at night.

He did a turn in it, then jumped out again.

She hoped that when the lights were out, he'd remember the box.

Max fussed until after ten. They took turns walking him, bouncing him, playing with him on a blanket on the floor. He would be distracted for a few minutes, then whine and cry again.

"A tooth, probably," Sal guessed as he lay stretched out on the sofa, while Dori paced. "I was vacationing with Diego and Manuela when Rosa was teething. I suppose it won't make you feel any better to warn you that there'll be no peace for months?"

"Thank you," she said with an amused glance at him. She turned and paced in the other direction. "No, it doesn't. I was hoping maybe he just got overly excited about the cat. I remember Mom telling Skye that babies sometimes get themselves so excited and overtired, they don't know how to calm down." Skye was Darrick's wife.

"And whiskey is not the answer?"

"No, it isn't. It's being calm and calming them."

"I'm calm," Sal said, "but he's still fussing."

Dori laughed. "I have about two more minutes of calm left, then I'm going to start screaming myself."

Sal swung his feet to the floor. "Then, it must be my turn to pace."

"Oh…oh…" she said quietly, stopping in her tracks and looking over the baby's head at Sal. "Look," she whispered.

Max's head lolled against her shoulder, then finally fell back into the crook of her arm as he went to sleep.

She remained where she stood and rocked him back and forth for a few minutes until satisfied that he was well and truly asleep.

She smiled wearily at Sal. "Thank goodness," she

said softly. "I'm going to bed, too. See you in the morning."

"Okay." He blew her a kiss.

She responded with a tilt of her chin in his direction, wondering, had her hands been free, if she'd have blown one back.

Max slept until just after three.

"Almost four hours' sleep in a row," Dori thought, reaching for the bottle of juice she'd placed in a small cooler under the bedside table.

Then she remembered that during their frantic effort last evening to calm Max, she'd come upstairs for the bottle of juice because there had been none left in the refrigerator.

She picked Max up, wrapped him in his blanket and went quietly down the stairs to the kitchen. She took one of the bottles Sal had run through the dishwasher that afternoon, filled it with milk and ran it under the hot water tap.

Max took it eagerly, wrapping both little hands around it. She walked around the side of the kitchen and into the pantry to check Cheddar's box and was disappointed to find it empty.

Where had he gone? she wondered, hoping he wasn't scratching furniture or doing other rude things in her brothers' house.

It was as she turned back to the kitchen that she saw the face in the window. It was peering in the top half of the back door. If it weren't for the whites of the eyes, she thought as she stared, horrified, at the picture it made framed by the window, she might not have noticed it. The face looked as though it had been blackened. The eyes had a wide, frenzied look.

She watched in terror as the doorknob turned, first one way, then the other. She opened her mouth to scream—at that moment, Sal flew out of the bedroom, yanked the door open and ran out into the night.

"Sal, no!" she shouted after him, but he was already gone.

With shaking fingers, she dialed 911. A young man's calm voice told her help would be there soon.

Sal was back in two minutes. "Are you all right?" he demanded, putting one hand to her face and the other to Max's.

"He didn't get in," she said, her voice trembling. "Did you see him?"

He shook his head. "He jumped the back fence, and I didn't want to get too far away on the chance there was someone else with him, just waiting for me to disappear."

The police arrived a moment later. Sal took one of them outside to show him the path the "face" had taken, while Dori told the other officer what had happened. He took notes, then excused himself to return a call from the station on the radio transmitter clipped to his shoulder.

"Apparently one of your neighbors a block down the hill just called in a prowler." He smiled sympathetically. "He's probably looking for an unlocked door," he said. "I know that was frightening, but now that he knows there's a man in the house, I doubt he'll bother you again. Most prowlers get off on scaring women alone."

Dori nodded politely, thinking it probably hadn't been a simple prowler, but proof of Sal's theory about someone wanting their money back. But she knew she couldn't say anything about that.

Sal walked in from the back with the other officer.

"And your name?" the officer who'd questioned her asked.

She suddenly realized that she was dealing with legalities here, with someone who would probably track records down and learn things she'd never told anyone.

"Dorianne McKeon..." She hesitated a moment as she caught Sal's eye and added with a sense of having just turned her entire life upside down, "Dominguez."

Sal raised an eyebrow.

"And you, sir?"

"Salvatore Dominguez," Sal replied.

"I'm glad you're vigilant, Mr. Dominguez," said the officer who'd followed him outside. "But it might be a good idea to call us first, before you follow a prowler into the night."

Sal nodded agreement, never mentioning what he did for a living.

"I told your wife," the other officer said, "that prowlers seldom come back when they know there's a man in the house. And we'll keep driving through the neighborhood during the night."

"Thank you," Sal said, walking them to the door. "And we appreciate your quick response."

"Sure. Good night, now."

"Good night."

Sal closed and locked the door, hooked the chain in place, then turned to Dori with a smile. "I'm sorry you were frightened, *querida*," he said, putting a hand to her cheek. "But that was the first time I've been able to enjoy hearing you call yourself by your rightful name. Come." He put an arm around her shoulders. "I'll make you some tea."

CHAPTER SEVEN

"WHERE'S CHEDDAR?" Dori asked, trying to avoid a discussion of her name.

Sal pointed to the open door of his room as he passed it on his way to the kitchen. Dori peered inside and saw Cheddar on his side on the bed's second pillow, one paw over his eyes, the toes on his hind feet curled in.

"It's a good thing we didn't take him in hoping for an attack cat." Dori looked around for the bottle of milk she'd prepared before she'd been frightened by the face.

It lay in the middle of the kitchen floor, still tightly closed. She picked it up, and Max reached for it, screeching his disapproval when she put it in the sink and started over with a fresh bottle and more milk.

She finally sat at the kitchen table with it, Max in the crook of her arm sucking hungrily.

She was trembling. She felt it inside, a sort of quivering in her stomach that seemed to grow with her memory of the face in the window, until her whole body was shaking.

She couldn't remember ever feeling so frightened. But then, she'd never been responsible for the safety of a baby before.

She rocked Max, hoping the action would hide from Sal that she was quavering.

"What made you come running?" she asked, mistakenly thinking that making conversation would contribute to the illusion that she was fine despite the scare. "I never got a chance to scream." She was pleased. The question came out sounding strong, interested.

"I heard you come downstairs," he replied, pulling cups down from the cupboard as water began to heat in the kettle. He reached for her box of tea. "Then I heard him outside. I've been expecting some kind of…"

He glanced in her direction as he held up a box of cookies, apparently to ask her if she wanted one with her tea.

She tossed her hair back, a casual gesture that might have worked had she had hair to toss. As it was, it just seemed to punctuate her fear with a giant exclamation point.

He put the box down on the counter and walked past her into the living room, then returned with a cotton throw that he wrapped around her shoulders, tucking the back in between her and the chair.

He fell to one knee in front of her to adjust it around the baby. Then he looked into her eyes.

"I promise you," he said earnestly, "that I won't let anything happen to you or Max. This is what I do, Dori. You're safe."

She nodded, fighting the need to burst into tears. But that wouldn't advance her plan for the summer.

Not that anything that had happened in the past few days was doing anything at all for the plan.

"I know," she said, her voice strained. "It's just that the face in the window was...scary." She held the baby more tightly. "I wonder how he knows I have the money?"

"Did you see one face or two?" He wiped a tear away with his thumb.

She hadn't realized she'd let one fall.

"Just one. Why? Did you see two people?"

"No, I chased just one," he replied. "But I heard something in the bushes on the other side of the yard. Could have been raccoons, or possums."

"Or Max's mother is hooked up with her boyfriend again," Dori speculated, "and wants her baby back."

"Anything's possible. But for now, you just have to relax. Sit tight, and I'll put some brandy in your tea."

She watched in perplexity a few moments later when he carried the tea into his bedroom rather than to the table.

"Come on into my room," he said, returning to turn off the kitchen light. "I'll feel better if the two of you are in sight."

She followed him a little hesitantly, not sure this was a good idea. It was also contrary to what he'd said in the beginning—but he probably guessed that she did not want to be alone with Max upstairs.

He had propped up the pillows, and now pointed her to the side away from the window. Cheddar had been moved to the seat of a wicker chair and didn't seem to mind.

"You have your tea, I'll finish feeding Max." Max never missed a beat with his bottle, while Sal took him from Dori. "When you're finished, I'll go get his crib and bring it down here."

They sat leaning against the headboard, Sal with the baby in his arms, Dori sipping her tea, and talked about everything but what had happened tonight.

She didn't care for the taste of the spiked tea, but it did blaze a nice warm trail into her stomach, where that betraying tremor originated. It was quieting now. She was still afraid, but better able to cope.

"Have you called the lawyer?" Sal asked.

Max had finished the contents of his bottle and yawned mightily. Sal put him to his shoulder and patted his back.

"No," Dori admitted. "I got to wondering what the law would require her to do if she knew I had a baby that wasn't mine. Maybe she'd have to tell Adult and Family Services."

"I'm not sure," Sal replied, "but I think if you'd hired her, that's privileged information. And considering how you got him—I mean, you've got that letter with your name on it that proves the parent intended you to have him—I think you'd be safe."

She might be, but she didn't want to take the chance.

"I'll just wait until this is all over." She turned to Sal, comforted by the muscular arm wrapped around the baby, the strong, bare legs in jogging shorts stretched out atop the covers. "But how are we going to get to the bottom of it?"

"I'm working on it," he replied. The baby belched

loudly, and Sal turned to grin at Dori. "I hired a private detective," he added.

She blinked at him. "Why didn't you tell me?"

"Because everything was fine, your work on your book was going well. I didn't want you to worry if you didn't have to."

"Did you hire someone from town?"

"Yes."

"Not Bram Bishop?"

"Yes. Husband of a friend of yours. He told me." He laughed lightly. "Small-town life. Everybody's connected somehow. Which worked in our favor, because it turns out that *his* brother-in-law, who has a photo studio, was taking a passport photo for a couple that provide flowers for the church—and they told the photographer, who told Bishop, that the young housekeeper who was just hired at the church in February has been missing since the theft. So he's on her trail."

"Do you think it's Max's mother?" she asked.

"I don't know. We'll have to be patient and see what he comes up with. I'll call him in the morning and tell him about tonight."

"But it was a man's face I saw in the window," she insisted.

"Which proves my theory that she's probably working with or for a boyfriend."

Max belched again and began to make little melodic sounds, as though wanting to be part of the conversation.

Dori put her empty cup aside and turned toward Sal to rub Max's back. "I wonder if he's trying to tell us he thinks his mother is innocent."

"Guys always think their mother is innocent."

Sal smiled, a little ruefully, she thought.

Dori tried to remember what little she knew about Sal's mother. She'd died very young, and her absence had been Sal's father's impetus to follow his brother-in-law into a life as a jewel thief.

"You were twelve when your mother died," Dori said.

He nodded, stroking the baby's back.

Dori waited for him to volunteer more. He didn't.

Suspecting there was something important here, she persisted gently, "You've never talked about her very much."

"I know." He sighed. "I discovered she wasn't perfect one day when I was about ten years old, and in my foolish youth, that was hard to take."

"Another man?" she guessed.

He leaned back against the pillows and stared at the ceiling. "My father's friend, Mateo Salvatore. She had his baby when I was eleven."

"You're named after him?"

"Yes."

Dori leaned her cheek against his shoulder, wondering why he'd kept that from her all this time. Then she remembered that it wasn't the kind of thing one shared on first meeting. Their early relationship had consisted of quick, clandestine rendezvous, and that night at the Plaza when things had been passionate one moment, then frantic when they'd made the quick flight to Florida.

They'd quarreled and separated. Then she'd run to him in Mexico—and those days before the wedding had been spent catching up, making promises, planning the future. Not resurrecting the past.

"If it still hurts you," she encouraged softly, "it might help to share it."

"It's been over a long time," he said.

"But you sound as though it still matters."

He closed his eyes and drew a deep breath. Max rose and fell with Sal's chest, now fast asleep against him.

"She was very beautiful and very gentle," he said, slowly reeling out the memory, "and later, when I understood him as a man, I realized that my father was strong and did his best to provide for us. But he was very exacting, sometimes to the point of forgetting that children learned by making mistakes. And people, too. I think my mother's life must have been dull and hard and without much laughter."

He paused and patted Max when he wriggled, then settled down again. "One day my mother wasn't there when I woke up, and my father told me what had happened, that she was expecting Mateo's baby and they had run away together."

"Oh, Sal." She wrapped her arms around him.

"Mateo left her destitute somewhere in Juarez some time later. He was smuggled over the border with a dozen others and died in the back of a pickup in a traffic accident."

"What happened to your mother?"

"She came back to us, about to have the baby. To my father's credit, he let her stay, but he refused to raise the baby. When the child was born, my mother turned it over to a priest, who found an adoptive family in Mexico City. She was broken in spirit and lived with the guilt of what she'd done every day. She died the next year."

"Sal, I'm so sorry." She hugged him, trying desperately to find some hope in that sad story.

"But...you might have a brother somewhere," she said. "Have you looked into it?"

He smiled a little grimly. "I have a sister," he said, then added quietly, "Desideria."

Dori started upright, unable to believe she hadn't seen that coming. *Desideria.* She felt as though she'd been punched hard, then dunked in cold water.

She'd left her husband because he'd gone to the rescue of...his sister, she thought in disbelief.

"She was raised by a wealthy family who were happy to receive my letter, explaining who I was and that I thought I was their daughter's brother. I promised that I wouldn't intrude, that I just wanted to know that she was well."

He smiled. "Her mother wrote back that she was not only well, but beautiful, intelligent and prone to be wild. Desi's adopted father had died, and her mother was worried about her. She invited me to visit.

"I did, we all got on famously, and I became a part of Desi's life. She unfortunately had a predilection for falling in love with dangerous men and eventually married a man who conducted just the kind of business that had killed Mateo.

"I received a frightened call from her one day when she suspected what his export business truly was, and together we alerted the border guards and finally sent him to jail. At the time of our wedding, he got away during an accident while he was being transported from one prison to another, and he headed back to Laredo to exact revenge against Desi for sending him to jail.''

Dori looked into his eyes and saw no anger there, no resentment, no grudge against her, just fear at the memory of the danger his sister had faced.

I left him, she thought in disbelief, *because he went to save his sister's life.*

She sat still, trying to absorb what she'd done. Anguished over his perception of her as someone he could walk away from, to run to the rescue of a beautiful young woman she'd heard was reckless and spoiled. Dori had fled. And she'd refused to listen to the truth when he'd followed her home—she'd been so sure she knew all she had to know.

Oh, God.

SO. THE TRUTH was out. Sal looked into Dori's face and suspected that this wasn't necessarily a good thing. She'd finally asked to hear the truth that he should have shared earlier, the truth he had tried to explain when he'd come home from Texas, then had given up on for the two years he and Dori were apart.

But judging now by the astonished, guilt-ridden look in her eyes, it was going to do him more harm than good.

"I'm sorry," she said finally, her dark eyes wide and stricken. "You didn't tell me..."

He nodded. "Before we got married," he said, "we had so many other things to talk about. And afterward, you wouldn't listen."

"I thought she was a friend," she whispered. "She was introduced to me as a friend of yours! No one in Madre Maria knew she was your sister."

"She wanted it that way. In the States, when her husband was arrested, there was a lot of scandal attached to their name. She wanted to help out at the hospital, but she didn't want any of that notoriety to touch the project, so she came with a phony last name—and as a friend."

"She looked at you with such adoration!"

He shrugged. "The way you look at Duncan or Darrick or Dillon. They've loved you and rescued you, and you love them for it."

She put both hands to her face.

Sal put the baby down on the bed between them and swung his legs out of bed. "I'll go get the crib. If we don't get some sleep, we won't even hear him wake up."

He ran lightly up the stairs, wondering how best to handle this. If he was forgiving and understanding, she would slip deeper into that well of guilt and self-flagellation.

But he didn't have the heart to remind her that she'd robbed them of two years of their life together. It would certainly make her feel anger rather than guilt, but he couldn't do it.

He picked up the portable crib from the room she occupied upstairs and carried it down. There had to be a middle ground, he thought, between rubbing it in and letting her off.

When he walked into the downstairs bedroom, Dori

sat in the middle of the bed, Cheddar in her lap, the baby beside her still sound asleep.

Sal scooped Max up, lay him in the crib and covered him with the blue blanket. He turned off the light and climbed into bed beside her with a casual ease he was far from feeling.

She didn't move. "Sal?" she asked after a moment.

"Yes?"

"I don't want this to be my fault." Her voice was tight and high. "I...was so sure it was yours."

"I know. Forget it."

"How can I forget it? I cost us two years of our marriage!"

And that was where he found the solution. It was drastic, and it would hurt, but it might also work. And it would take the pressure off and give them time.

"Doesn't matter anymore," he said genially. "You said so yourself, and I'm beginning to think you're right. Now that we've both decided there's nothing left, it doesn't really matter how it fell apart. Relax. I've got my business, you've got your book."

There was a long, heavy silence from her side of the bed. Then she slid down under the covers. Her heel collided with his hip as she lay down, and he felt a very familiar twang of desire.

"Sorry," she said.

"No problem," he assured her. Oh, yeah. This was another one of his good ideas.

"Good night," she said.

He turned onto his back. "Bacon and eggs for breakfast?" he asked.

"Sure," she replied in a small voice.

Something touched his arm, and he had an instant of hopeful expectation. Then he heard the rumble of an enthusiastic cat purr and was suddenly trod upon by four padded feet. They did a circle on his chest and suddenly sat, sharp little teeth biting his chin in a cat kiss.

"Your cat's on me," he said.

He heard Dori's sigh in the darkness. "He must have liked the sound of bacon and eggs for breakfast, too."

"We have to get some cat food tomorrow." She sounded grim, and he thought a simple domestic conversation might lighten her mood. "And litter, probably."

"Yeah. And I have to find something for my mom's birthday. She'll be sixty-three next week."

"That should be easy. There's that big antique shop downtown. They're still collectors, aren't they?"

"Yes, but you know my parents' reputation for falling in love with ugly stuff. We may have to travel around to find something bad enough for Mom to appreciate."

"We'll do that. It's good to have a purpose."

There was no response from her side of the bed.

Sal closed his eyes and tried to sleep, not an easy task with her just a hand-span away.

Without warning, she sat up again. "What do you mean, we've decided it doesn't matter?"

Cheddar, startled by the sudden movement, leaped off him.

Knowing this was a critical question, Sal considered his answer.

Dori poked his shoulder, apparently wondering if he'd heard her. "Are you awake?"

"Of course, I'm awake." He propped up on an elbow, facing her. He couldn't see her in the darkness, but all his radar told him she was there. "I didn't say we decided it didn't matter—I said it didn't matter because we've decided there's nothing left."

"Who's decided?" she demanded.

"I believe it was you," he replied. "You couldn't love someone who took vows one minute and walked away from them the next, so—"

"But I didn't know the truth when I said that."

"Not my fault. I asked Diego to explain it to you. But you didn't listen. Then I went to your place when I came home, to try to tell you about it, but again, you—"

"You'd left me on our wedding day!"

"Here we go again." He flung a hand out in exasperation and made contact with her bare arm. He drew his hand back, everything connected to it pulsing in reaction.

"I'm sorry about what happened," she said plaintively. "You just don't understand what I was feeling when you left. You just know you had a noble reason and that makes you right, and I'm just a selfish brat because I was hurt."

"No, you were a selfish brat," he amended carefully, "because you wouldn't listen to an explanation."

"Fine." He felt her slam back against her pillow. "I don't want to talk about it anymore."

Maybe letting her be eaten by guilt, he thought with fresh frustration, wouldn't have been so unpalatable, after all.

The next three days passed in the same way. They were polite and considerate of each other. He prepared meals and watched the baby in the morning so she could work, and she cleaned up and watched Max in the afternoon so Sal could check with the office, do a few chores around the garden, and lay out in the hammock, nothing more productive on his agenda.

They slept side by side at night, never touching, and Cheddar slept between them on the pillows. Max woke only once a night, and whoever was awake responded. They had domesticity down to an art. They just couldn't find the bliss.

IT DIDN'T MATTER.

There was nothing left.

When she wasn't writing, Dori played those lines over and over in her head. The basic truth was that it was all *her fault* that it didn't matter and that there was nothing left.

She spent long hours in the afternoon thinking about it, Max in the playpen while she cleaned house. She'd tried to remember every detail so that she could put the blame elsewhere. But it stood squarely with her.

So it was up to her to fix it.

But how did you re-engage the affections of a man whom you had alienated sufficiently that he could finally bare his soul—then tell you the loss of your love didn't matter because there was nothing left of his?

Then the obvious occurred to her.

It was early Saturday evening and she'd just put Max down after a napless day. Sal lay in the bathtub soaking away an entire afternoon of mowing, trimming, pulling weeds and filling a large terracotta pot with pink begonias, while alyssum and blue lobelia. The flower-filled pot was a gift for her mother that she intended to deliver the following week when she visited for her birthday. The search for the perfect "ugly" antique continued.

Sal had emerged from the garden, moaning. Dori had helped him off with his shirt. "You're a little rickety for thirty-six, aren't you?" she teased.

He groaned as he pulled his arm out of a sleeve and gave her an injured look. "I've been spending a lot of time at a desk for almost two years."

Her eyes roamed over his shoulders as she prepared to tease him again, then she saw a ragged scar on the front of his right shoulder and an elongated one from collar bone to rotator cuff on the left. The long one was still thick and corded, and looked as though, whatever the cause, it had been painful.

She put her fingertips to the ragged scar. "What happened here?" she asked.

"A bullet," he replied, his voice a little weak.

She remembered reading about his defense of a newspaper man who'd uncovered corruption in Seattle's City Hall. He'd defended the man, she remembered, by blocking the bullet. "That newspaper man?"

"No, that's the other shoulder. This one is from Paco."

"Who's Paco?"

He answered cautiously. "Desi's husband."

She'd seen him without his shirt during those days before the wedding. He'd worked bare-chested in the hospital, and he cooked that way at home in the intense heat. She remembered what a flawlessly beautiful specimen he'd been. It wasn't that she considered him diminished by the wounds, but she felt personally affronted that such a thing could have happened to him, that someone else would have deliberately hurt him in such a way. It made her feel vengeful and darkly angry.

"Well, goodness, Sal," she said, trying to force lightness into her voice. "Certainly you must have another technique for protecting people than acting as a shield? You're out of shoulders. What will you sacrifice next?"

He struggled with a smile, apparently amused by her reaction. "I don't know," he replied. "What do you think I could do without?"

She stood on tiptoe to rap her knuckles lightly on his head. "This doesn't seem to be doing you much good. Climb into the bathtub, and I'll bring you some wine."

That was why it had taken him seven days to come home from Desi's, she thought as she went into the kitchen. He'd probably spent that time recovering from the wound.

She took a bottle of Reisling from the refrigerator and filled a wineglass three-quarters full. She put Max in his carrier and walked wine and baby upstairs, then put Max near the bed in the room they'd occupied across the hall from the bathroom.

Wine in hand, she rapped lightly on the half-open bathroom door.

"Come in," Sal said, the tone of his voice suggesting uncertainty.

She walked in and handed him the glass. He was covered to the middle of his chest in the aromatherapy suds she'd put into the water, and he raised a bubbly hand to take the glass from her.

"Thank you," he said. He took a sip and leaned back with an appreciative sigh.

"You want me to fix dinner?" she asked, reaching for the loofa and the soap on the dish near the faucet. She dipped the sponge into the water to get it wet.

Eyes closed, he smiled. "Please, *querida*. Haven't I suffered enough?"

"I should splash you," she replied, coming around behind him, "but you don't look as though you could defend yourself. Want your back scrubbed?"

He was still for a moment, and she thought he might refuse. Then he sat forward and allowed her access. "Where's the baby?" he asked.

"In his carrier right across the hall," she replied. "Fast asleep."

She rubbed soap onto the wet sponge and began to work it slowly from shoulder to shoulder. Neither bullet, she noticed in relief, had penetrated his back.

"Then going out wouldn't be wise. We could call for pizza, or I could get Chinese takeout."

"Pizza's a good idea," she said, a little distracted

by the definition of his back muscles. She watched them move as he brought the wine to his mouth.

She worked the sponge in circles down his spinal column, dipping into the water to follow the ridges of vertebrae.

The man she'd teased just a moment ago about being defenseless turned and caught her arm and hauled her across the tub so that she sat suspended over the water, her legs straight out ahead of her and resting on the rim.

She squealed in surprise.

"Would you like to get wet?" It was a threat, not a question. The look in his eyes said she had his complete attention.

"Depends," she replied, relaxing in his arms. "What's in it for me, if I do?"

His voice lowered an octave. "What are you after, *corazón?*"

She met and held his gaze. "You, my love."

There was surprise in his eyes for an instant, then passion ignited there. "You have always had me. You just kept too great a distance between us."

"That's not a problem now," she pointed out.

He lowered her into his lap, put a hand behind her head to protect her from collision with the wall, and kissed her soundly while his free hand unfastened the buttons of her shirt.

Warm water soaked through her clothes from her bottom to her breasts.

She had him now.

HE SHOULD ASK QUESTIONS, he thought drunkenly, as she returned his kisses with ardent eagerness.

There was something in her eyes that troubled him, something that didn't seem entirely...spontaneous. Not that there was anything wrong with a planned seduction. He just couldn't help wondering what had changed her mind so completely.

If this was sympathy over his wounds, or some kind of compensation for having left him, he didn't want it. Oh, hell, who was he kidding? Of course he wanted it, whatever motivated her.

Once he had her buttons undone, he sat her forward to help her pull off the shirt. Her sports bra came off right over her head, leaving two perfect little globes, rose-tipped and beading, as he leaned down to kiss one and then the other.

He turned her lengthwise atop him so that she could shed her elastic-waisted shorts and panties, then he cradled her again. But before he could claim her mouth, she smiled and pointed to her shoes and socks.

"You can drown in the water—" she giggled "—wearing shoes and socks."

"Don't worry," he said, his brain barely functioning enough to form words now that her bare flesh was against his, "we'll keep you on top."

She toed off the shoes, and he reached a hand out to pull off the socks. Then he turned her onto her stomach atop him.

For a moment they simply held each other. Then she squirmed against him, as if to get closer still, her arms tight around his neck as though he was the answer to a prayer.

He framed her face in his hands and saw the love in her eyes, the small smile. She put her hands over his and said with a wince, "I should probably tell you…"

He put a fingertip to her lips. "No confessions. I've done things *I* even prefer not to know."

She kissed his fingertip, then lowered it, a little frown still in place. "I was just going to confess virginity," she said.

CHAPTER EIGHT

THERE'D BEEN MOMENTS before they were married when he'd suspected that. She'd had a kind of innocence in her glance and in her touch that he didn't think would be there if she'd had experience.

But then he'd told himself he was imagining things. She'd been the protected younger sister of three watchful brothers, but she'd been abroad to school, she'd traveled extensively on her own doing research for her work. And she was beautiful and desirable. There had to have been someone.

"At twenty-six, *querida?*" he asked.

Arms wrapped around his neck, she sat sideways and brought her knees up so that she was curled in his lap.

"I was a serious scholar, with brothers who looked over my friends and checked out my boyfriends. Those brave enough to date me a second time were not brave enough to do anything but kiss me goodnight—and usually on the forehead."

Sal smiled at that. He'd been investigated, he knew. Despite his background as a thief, the McKeons had approved him. It was Dori who'd been the holdout.

"Then I met you," she went on, "and even though you went back to Mexico and things looked impossible for us, you were on my mind all the time." She smiled. "Then I chased you down, and we planned to get married in the Church and that meant we had to wait to make love."

That had been torturous because he'd insisted that Dori stay at his home where conditions were more comfortable than in the little cantina in town.

"My housekeeper watched us like a hawk," he recalled with a light laugh. Then he grew serious again. "But that was two years ago."

"Yes," she admitted, "but I've been a married woman since then." She tucked the tip of her slender index finger into the center of the small hoop earring on her left ear. "Doesn't this look familiar to you?"

He took it in his hand, careful not to pull. His heart punched against his ribs when he saw the thin inscription inside it. *Mi amor,* it said simply. My love.

"This is your wedding ring!" he said, freeing her ear and turning her chin toward him. "Why?"

"Because I loved you," she said grudgingly, "but I was so angry at you for leaving me. I didn't want to wear your ring, but I couldn't put it in a drawer, either. So I found another hoop that matched and made my wedding ring into an earring."

He'd intended an impromptu lovemaking in the tub, thinking the unorthodox setting would be part of the fun of finally coming together.

But she was a virgin. And she'd always loved him. He'd be damned if her first time would be in a bathtub.

He lifted her out of the water again, propping her

bottom on the rim. "We're rethinking this," he said, pulling himself to his feet.

"I don't *want* to rethink it!" she complained. "I've been planning this all afternoon!"

He snatched a towel off the rack and handed it to her, then took one for himself. "I've been planning it longer than that," he said with a quick kiss. He dried himself off, then wrapped the towel around his waist. "I don't mean we aren't going to make love. We're just not going to do it in the tub."

He took the towel from her, dried her back and her hips, almost driving himself over the edge when he wrapped it around her and tucked it above her breast.

He lifted her into his arms and walked across the hallway with her into the bedroom she'd occupied with the baby. Max was still asleep in the carrier.

"Do you think we could pretend," she asked as he set her down by the side of the bed, "that two years *haven't* passed, that it's our wedding day and we've made it all the way back to your place where there's the scent of jacarandas coming in through the window?"

He tossed the covers back on the bed, then hooked a finger in her towel to pull it off, dropping his own as well.

"We can pretend whatever you want," he said, lifting her again to place her in the middle of the bed. "But this is very nice." He pointed to the lace curtains blowing into the room on an early evening breeze. "I smell roses and the salty fragrance of the ocean. And you."

Sal lay down beside her and nuzzled her throat.

"That complicated fragrance that haunted my place for weeks after you left. Lavender and..."

"Vanilla," she whispered.

"Mmm. It's in my black sweater now," he said, turning onto his side and wrapping her in his arms. "You're all over me, Dori. Inside, outside, everywhere."

"Good." She kissed his throat as he began to explore the line of her back, the flare of her hip. "I want us to be forever entangled. Not a fairy-tale romance, but the real thing—where you're so close you're not entirely sure who's who, and it lasts forever."

He caught the back of her thigh and pulled her leg over him so that he could chart her from knee to torso. "It's been the real thing for me since the first time I saw you."

She tipped her head back to smile at him. "I thought you were gorgeous but autocratic."

"I was trying to protect Julie's father."

"And I was trying to explain Julie's position."

"Then their relationship was restored thanks to us, and *we* couldn't get along."

"We're getting along now," she said with a little sigh as she dropped her head against his shoulder. "Tell me what to do for you, *querido*."

He held her closer, loving the sound of the old endearment on her tongue. "Do whatever occurs to you, my heart, and I will love it."

WHAT SHE WANTED TO DO, Dori thought, was to learn everything about his magnificent body. She touched him everywhere, letting her fingertips trace the outline of his shoulders and arms, follow the ridge of his collar bone and ribs, explore the tangled pattern of chest hair that ran down his chest, past his waist, over his flat abdomen, to the juncture of his thighs.

He caught her hand before she could touch his manhood. "Not yet," he said with a self-deprecating little laugh, "or there won't be time for all I want you to know."

He pushed her gently onto her back, his hands doing just what hers had done to him, except that he seemed inordinately skilled—everywhere he touched seemed to acquire a life she'd never been aware of. Her breasts tingled; shudders rippled under her rib cage and inside her belly.

His lips followed his fingertips, and her body arched toward him of its own volition, as though it no longer needed instructions from her.

The notion was both liberating and alarming. But he made her feel too wonderful for her to be afraid of anything. Her only regret was that she'd missed two whole years of this!

He tucked her into his arm and reached gently inside her. She lay very still, focused on the exquisite rightness of his tender invasion. As his hand moved gently and her body accustomed itself to his exploration, the scholar in her thought to analyze the nature of a woman's react—

A tight spiral of feeling began deep inside, and she lost all powers of analysis. Thought fled. That tight little feeling began to grow and recede, grow and recede, until she felt a sort of frantic desperation to catch it, to know what it was.

"Easy," he coached quietly. "Just be easy."

"I want to touch you!" she said urgently. It would help. She knew it would help.

"Not yet," he insisted. "Focus on you. Think about you."

She opened her mouth to protest, but only a small, startled gasp escaped, as pleasure darted at her one more time, then broke over her in a shockingly intense wave.

She felt powerless to move, pinned against the mattress with pleasure. So that was the truth everyone else knew. The magic wasn't just in that star-shower of feeling, but in the fact that a loving and caring man could give it to you.

As her pleasure subsided, what occurred to her first was the need to return that unutterable sense of well-being. "Salvatore!" she whispered earnestly, running her hands down the middle of his stomach.

"No," he cautioned, trying to stop her. "Not until— Ah!"

She closed her hand over him with a reverence for all he'd just given her.

"Dori, I said..." He sat up again to try to stop her, but she pushed him back, her forearm leaning on his chest as she said sweetly, "Easy, *querido*. Focus on yourself. Think about yourself."

Caressing him was all new to her, but there was clear evidence that she could be very good at this.

She was just beginning to feel confidence when he caught her by the waist and lifted her astride him.

"All right," he said, his voice strained. "I wanted to give you more time, but if you insist on being in control, you must now be in control of all of me."

He caught her hips in his hands to brace her as he lifted up, poised to enter her.

She smiled. "Then let me have all of you. I've waited forever."

He thrust upward, and they came together at last.

For just an instant the pressure felt like more than she could bear. A metaphor for their lives, she thought. She'd always felt as though he filled her life too full, as though she couldn't contain him without losing herself.

Then, as had happened when he'd first come home with her, a certain satisfaction in his presence eased the discomfort, then the satisfaction turned to contentment, the contentment to happiness and the happiness to a joy so profound that she could hold him easily. And she wondered how she'd managed this long without him.

Then clever metaphors fled, basic thought fled, as pleasure came at her again—bigger, deeper, more sweeping.

She began to move on him, some instinct making her sway in a little circle.

He laced his hands in hers to give her leverage. Then they were moving together, and this time she didn't have to pursue fulfillment—it hit her broadside so that her head fell back even as she tightened her knees and her fingers to hold on.

SAL HAD NEVER had an experience like this, in which a partner's pleasure gave him the delicious thrill he felt now. She'd been so determined to be in control, and was now enslaved to him.

Of course, he was securely bound and shackled himself, as she seemed to dissolve with pleasure, arch backward with release, then collapse atop him with a long, ragged sigh. He freed himself, lifted her off him, then gathered her in his arms.

"Oh, Sal," she groaned against his chest.

"I know," he said, still adjusting to the miracle of having made love to her. "Tell me we weren't destined for each other."

"I hate to think of the time wasted," she said regretfully.

"Then, don't." He gave the back of her hair a little tug. "Think of all that lies ahead. Babies, that house up the hill from the theater, growing old together—"

There was a sudden scratching on the other side of the bedroom door.

Dori looked up in the direction of the carrier. "What is that?" she asked. "Max is still asleep."

"Cheddar has found us," Sal guessed. "Now we not only have to contend with making sure the baby's asleep so we can make love, but we have to sedate the cat."

"About more babies…" she said, obviously not concerned about the cat.

"You don't like the idea?" he asked worriedly.

"Oh, no. I love it," she assured him. "But I was thinking about Max. I mean, that's okay with you, isn't it? Keeping him? Adopting him?"

"Of course. I love him as much as you do."

She sighed and rested her head on his shoulder again. "Good. I'll be so glad when we know where we stand there. I hope Gusty's husband finds out something soon."

"Oh. Forgot to tell you," he said, wondering how he'd managed to do that. Although, as he remembered, he'd been one very frustrated man this afternoon. Hence the over-the-top yardwork. "Bram called while you were writing this morning, and we're invited to their place for lunch tomorrow."

"Really?"

"Really. He has some answers for us, and his wife's been cooped up with the baby all week. She thought it would be fun to have us over so that we can eat while we talk business, and the babies can play together."

She smiled, clearly pleased with the idea. "That sounds like fun. And Max will love it."

"All right. I was supposed to let him know. I'll call him back, then I'll call for pizza."

His timing impeccable, Max began to stir and shout to the world that he was awake. Beyond the door, the scratching grew frantic.

Dori groaned and pushed up on Sal's chest. "Darn it. Back to our real lives."

He pulled her back down for a quick kiss. "From now on, this *is* our real lives."

DORI LIVED in a state of wonder. They made love when they went to bed. They made love after getting Max back to sleep after a four a.m. feeding. They drove to Mass in Lincoln City, had brunch at the

Shilo Restaurant, then came home to relax for a few hours before going on to lunch—and made love again when Max dozed off.

If she'd known her marriage would be like this, she thought as she mixed a salad in Gusty's garage-apartment kitchen, she'd never have left for home two years ago.

Sal was turning out to be everything she'd ever prayed for in a husband. Though it was early yet, though the circumstances were unusual, and though she'd finally seen the light only one day ago, she had a good feeling about this. The marriage could work.

They ate steaks and salad at the Bishop's dining room table, while Max played with little Sadie on a blanket on the floor just beyond the table.

Sadie had the advantage. She was a mature nine-month-old who could sit up by herself, could use the bead rung on the side of the playpen to pull herself to a standing position, could take what she wanted to examine it, and could say "Mama." She was beautiful and seemed to delight in all she could do.

Max complacently allowed her to take his toys, and simply rolled and twisted away from her when she became too much of a pest.

"Brenda Ward, 18, is Max's mother," Bram said, consulting a sheet of notes near his plate on the table. "He was born on Valentine's Day in Lincoln City to Brenda and her boyfriend, Will Valdefiero. Valdefiero is a small-time hood who's always getting caught and doing time. He and Brenda met when they both worked for Burgers by the Sea."

Dori frowned over Max's sad beginning. "What's his full name?"

"Maximiliano Felipe Valdefiero," he replied, smiling. "Very important name for such a little guy. Police have been tracking the two. Brenda hasn't been back to work at the church since the theft."

"Are they sure *she* did it?"

"She probably just let the boyfriend in. His fingerprints were on the base of a lamp on the desk where the money was kept. He must have moved it for fear of knocking it over in the dark. The police are thinking they might still be around. The boy's car is still parked at Burgers. Nobody's seen the girl."

"Why would she help the boyfriend steal the money," Gusty asked, "then give it to Dori along with her baby? They must have had a falling out or something. If that's true, she has to be in big trouble with him."

"I hope he hasn't hurt her," Dori said, a little surprised that she'd said the words aloud. She smiled apologetically at her companions. "I think she cared for her baby."

"This note suggests that you know her," Bram said, as Gusty stacked plates.

Dori pushed her chair back to help, but Gusty gestured for her to remain seated. "You talk, I'll clear."

Dori focused on Bram. "I know, but I don't remember doing anything for anyone that would so convince them of my generosity that they'd give me their baby."

He held up a photo. "Does this jog your memory?"

She was shocked to recognize the face instantly. "It does!" she whispered in surprise, taking the photo from him and studying it. The memory unfolded easily. "But I only saw her once. In the rest room in the library. She had everything she owned in a backpack and she was washing her face." She could see the image as though it had happened that morning. "She must have been embarrassed to be caught doing that, because she told me she had a job interview at a church!" She turned abruptly to Bram, feeling mingled excitement and trepidation for the girl. "At a church!"

Tears sprang to her eyes, and she felt Sal's hand in the middle of her back, rubbing gently. "I heard her stomach growl," she continued, "and I gave her the chocolate bar I had in my purse." She was surprised by the wrench of emotion she felt. "That's all I did. One eighty-nine-cent chocolate bar."

"Street people," Sal said, "don't experience a lot of kindness. You touched her life, and for that moment you made a difference to her."

"And when she needed someone who'd love and care for her baby," Gusty said, her own eyes pooled with tears. "She thought of you."

"But I don't even live here," Dori said, surprised that the girl had found her. "I mean, I come and go a lot."

Bram shrugged. "You were here at the right time—both times."

Gusty hurried to retrieve Sadie as the baby ventured off the blanket and headed toward the television. "Anyone for dessert?" she asked, picking up

Sadie and placing her inside the playpen. "Chocolate torte with coffee ice cream. Show of hands."

Dori, thinking about Brenda Ward, missed the instructions. Sal raised her hand for her.

Sadie screamed a protest at being confined, while Gusty went to the kitchen. Gusty returned with a teething biscuit that she broke in half, giving one to each baby. Sadie began to munch, and quieted instantly.

Max fussed. Dori picked him up and gave him a bottle that kept him quiet while she ate dessert.

"Cliffside," Gusty said, pushing her dessert plate away and dabbing at her lips with a napkin, "is going to be crawling with babies by Christmas. Literally."

She referred to the property on which their garage apartment stood. It included the big house where Athena and her husband David and his brothers lived; a guest house once occupied by Alexis, the third triplet, and Trevyn McGinty, her husband, but now empty since they'd bought a house on the cove; and this apartment above the three-car garage.

"Athena told me she's pregnant," Dori said, pleased at the idea. It might make the attorney more determined to help her adopt Max.

"She is," Gusty replied. "And so's Alexis. They're due two weeks apart in November. Be ready to come to a baby shower sometime early in the fall." The sisters had married friends of Bram. The men had all once worked together in high-security government jobs.

"I'd love that," Dori said. "Our family's just blossoming with children. It's so much fun when we all get together to see who looks like whom and who's at what stage of development. My parents are so thrilled with their growing brood."

Gusty smiled wistfully. "Ours are gone, unfortunately. We have Bram's sister, though, and Trevyn's father, and, of course, David and Athena are raising David's younger brothers. Then we'll be adding two. Maybe the triplets and the McKeons will have to take a count and see who's ahead."

Dori thought about that remark later that night when she, Sal and Max had returned home. Sal walked the floor with the baby, who was fussy from all the excitement. Dori sat cross-legged on the sofa with McGinty's photo of her family in her lap. He had a photo studio now in the Bijou Theater building.

It had been taken on the beach just before a rainstorm. They'd all worn red and white, at her mother's request, and they were laughingly arm in arm, expecting to be rained on at any moment. There were children, babies, dogs—and a real air of happiness.

She counted heads.

"You don't have to bother," Sal said, pacing toward her with Max, who stood up stiffly in his arms, crying pitifully. Sal raised his voice to be heard. "We've got the numbers hands-down. You've got—what? Twelve, thirteen there?"

"Thirteen," she replied.

"Then Max and me. Fifteen."

She nodded. "Even with the babies coming in November, the triplets only have twelve counting Dottie."

"Dottie?"

"The housekeeper. I'm sure they'd count her."

"Then we're way ahead." He lifted the still-whining baby up in front of his face. "I'll bet you're crying because your mother looks so depressed. Maybe if you cheer up, she'll cheer up. What do you say?"

Max's response was to kick his feet and scream more loudly.

"That's what I thought." Sal put the baby on his shoulder again and continued walking. "I continue to be the only cool head around here."

"I was worrying about Brenda Ward," Dori admitted, holding the family photo to her chest. Her throat was thick, her eyes burning. "I want to keep Max more than anything, but what if she just made a stupid mistake and got hurt for it by the boyfriend? Or what if they find her and she wants Max back. Should she have another chance?"

Sal came to sit beside her, angled one leg on the other knee and placed the baby half on his thigh, half on the sofa. Max grew quiet, surprised by this new position. He took a fistful of Sal's pants leg and inched himself forward.

"You're asking big questions, Dori," Sal said, keeping a hand on Max's diapered bottom to steady his progress. "If she's committed a crime and has to go to jail, she'd lose the baby, at least for a time."

"I know. But what if she wants to straighten herself out? Maybe she regrets giving him to me."

Dori placed one of Max's toys on Sal's other knee, and the baby reached for it. "He's learning something new every day," she said, grimly thoughtful as she moved the toy within his reach. "He should have a good home. But should his mother lose everything because she screwed up?"

"You're wondering whether, if the situation comes up, you should go to court for custody," Sal spelled out for her.

She rested her cheek on Sal's shoulder as they played with the baby. "At first I thought I would. Now I wonder if it'd be the right thing to do."

"I guess you won't know that until she's found and you see what kind of young woman she is. If she put him in your car, it's entirely possible she's given him up in her heart, whatever happens."

"Yeah," Dori said. "'Cause I've accepted him in my heart."

"I know. And he adores you."

"And you. We'd be the perfect family."

He kissed the top of her head. "Let's not get upset about anything until we know for sure what we're dealing with, okay?"

She sighed. "I'd like to agree to that, but I know I'll worry, anyway."

Max managed to turn himself sideways, grab the front of Sal's shirt and grin broadly, pleased with himself.

"Whoa!" Sal said, sitting up and standing the baby on his knees.

"What?" Dori demanded worriedly, wondering what he'd seen. "What is it?"

Sal put an index finger to Max's bottom lip and drew it down until Dori saw the tiny rippled little bud of a tooth in the middle of his bottom gum.

She shrieked excitedly. "A tooth! He's got a tooth!"

Max, upset by her scream, began to cry again.

Sal turned to her with a teasingly condemning look. "Thanks, Mom. I've only been working on calming him down for an hour-and-a-half."

"Sorry," she said penitently, and took the baby from him. "Maybe a bath will do it. I did it, I'll fix it. You relax."

"You are a genius," Sal said half an hour later, when Max, bathed and toweled off and rocked, lay fast asleep in the crib in Sal's room.

She smiled. "Thank you. I've always maintained that myself, but I've had three brothers trying for years to prove me wrong. How about a cup of tea?"

"Already made," he said. He pointed to the teapot and cups on the coffee table.

They sank onto the sofa, sipped tea and watched television, all curled up together.

"I thought only old folks did this," she said tiredly.

He laughed. "I think children make you old."

"But you were talking about having more."

"I happen to like sitting with your legs in my lap and watching the Spice Channel. So I'm okay with it."

She backhanded him in the chest. "We're not watching the Spice Channel."

He held his cup of tea a safe distance away. "I was fantasizing a little. Want to go to bed and make my fantasies come true?"

"This would be the fourth time in the past twenty-four hours."

"Hah," he said. "That's why the triplets and their husbands will never catch up to the McKeon-Dominguez family."

"Oh, all right." She put her cup down, pretending reluctance. She stood and caught his hand. "If the honor of the family is at stake."

He went willingly. "Honor above all," he said heroically.

An hour later, Dori lay in his arms in the darkness and thought how lucky she was that Brenda Ward had put her baby in the back of Dori's car—because that had led Dori to contact Sal, which had led to this time together and finally to the rebirth of their marriage.

She owed Brenda a lot.

Dori had a second chance to rebuild her life after having selfishly almost destroyed it.

But didn't Brenda deserve a second chance as well?

CHAPTER NINE

MONDAY MORNING, Dori glanced at the calendar near her computer and noticed the big red circle around August third. Her brothers and their families would be home from Europe.

They had talked about using the beach house for a few days as a sort of leveling-out place before going back to their busy lives. They had also discussed celebrating their mother's August fifth birthday while here, and had told Dori that since she'd refused their invitation to accompany them to Europe, she could be in charge of preparations for the celebration.

She had to do something about that, she thought. And she had to brace herself to explain what Sal was doing here with her. She wondered if the living-together concept might not be easier to explain than the fact that they'd been married two years ago in a ceremony to which her family hadn't been invited.

She raised her hands from the keyboard and put them to her face with a groan. And then there was the baby. She could just imagine her parents' and her brothers' reactions to her decision not to go to the police.

She dropped her hands, squared her shoulders and focused on the hope that Bram would find Brenda by then. That way the entire matter of the money and the baby would be resolved.

And then she got the phone call. The voice was a raspy whisper. "Dori?"

She'd been rereading a line of dialogue as she picked up the receiver, but at the sound of the voice, she gave the call her complete attention. "Yes?" she asked.

There was a hesitation. Her heart began to race. "Brenda?" she asked.

A gasp sounded on the line. "How did you know it was me?" Then a little more pointedly, the woman added, "How did you know my name?"

Not a good move, Dori realized. Would Brenda suspect that she was being investigated?

She thought quickly. "I read the article in the paper about the theft from the church. It was exactly the same amount of money you left in the diaper bag. And no one's seen you since then, so that suggests you were involved." That detail hadn't been in the newspaper, but maybe Brenda wouldn't notice. "And it's clear from the note you left that the same person who left the baby, left the money."

Another pause, then a long breath. "How's Max?" the woman asked in a strained voice.

Dori felt everything inside her tense at the thought of the possibility that Brenda wanted Max back. "He's fine," she replied calmly. "I'm taking good care of him." She didn't want to ask, but she made herself do it. "Are you regretting giving him up?"

"No," Brenda replied with a quickness and sincerity that relieved Dori's mind. "I didn't like being a mother. He's a sweet baby, but I don't want him back."

That was chillingly firm.

"Do you still have the money?" Brenda asked her.

Dori tried to remember all Sal's cautions, but she couldn't help but worry about the frightened young woman on the phone.

"Did you steal it," she asked, "from whoever stole it from the church?"

There was another pause, then she replied in a frail voice, "Yes."

"Your boyfriend?"

"Yes."

"Does he know?"

There were sniffles, sighs. "He figured it out. Do you still have it?"

"Why?" Dori asked.

"Because if I can get it back," Brenda said, "and give it to the police, then maybe I won't have to go to jail when they catch Will. And I'll sign the release form so you can adopt Max without any trouble."

Dori's mind leaped ahead to the day Max did an adoption search and discovered that his mother had gone to jail for stealing from a church. She could protect him from that and secure his adoption at the same time.

"Where are you?" she asked.

"You still have it?" Brenda asked anxiously.

"Yes," Dori replied. "Where are you?"

"Can you meet me," Brenda asked, "in the corner of the park where that little bench sits under the big maple tree?"

Dori knew the one. It was concealed by a high hedge on one side and playground equipment on the other.

"What time?" Dori asked.

"Three o'clock?"

Dori looked at her watch. It was two-fifteen. "I'll be there," she said.

There was a pause, then Brenda said in a choked voice, "Thank you, Dori." And the line went dead.

Dori thought she knew just how to handle this.

She couldn't tell Sal what she was doing; that was clear. He'd be opposed to it, and either refuse to let her go or insist on coming along. Either reaction would result in her losing the opportunity to help Brenda.

But Sal worked in the yard every afternoon, with Max in the playpen under the shady ash. If Dori did this correctly, he wouldn't even know she was gone.

She hated to deceive him, but she knew he'd respond like the protector he'd made himself—and she had to do what she had to do.

She went downstairs on the pretext of filling the teakettle, an afternoon ritual. She stood in the doorway with it in hand and pushed open the screen door.

"Hi!" she called. "How're you two doing?"

Max, sitting up with a soft toy in his hand, squealed at the sight of her.

"Good." Sal looked up from the picnic table where he was working on his laptop, Cheddar curled up in a tight ball beside it. "Are you going to join us for an afternoon break?"

She shook her head regretfully, ignoring the little

pinch of guilt. "Sorry. I'm on a roll and I should probably stay with it. I just came down to refill my thermos. You want anything?"

He shook his head. "Not yet, thanks. Who called?"

"My mother," she replied, the pinch of guilt turning into an outright burn. "If I bring you the cordless, would you mind answering the phone for the rest of the afternoon, so I won't be distracted?"

"Of course not," he replied amiably.

She went back into the kitchen, put the empty kettle on the stove without turning on the burner, picked up the cordless phone from the kitchen counter and carried it outside.

Sal caught her wrist to pull her down for a quick kiss. "So your plot's coming together?" he asked.

She nodded, looking into his warm eyes and feeling suddenly fidgety and certain that the whole fake scenario showed in her face.

"Yeah," she replied, drawing away and taking a few backward steps toward the kitchen. "I'm fighting with the middle, but I think it's happening."

"Good." A very small wrinkle formed on his brow. "Don't fall over the playpen."

She turned to find the backs of her legs almost up against it. She rolled her eyes in self-deprecation, reached into the playpen, tickled Max—who giggled infectiously—then hurried back into the kitchen.

Her heart was pounding. *Good grief,* she thought. *Remind me never to embark on a life of crime.* She simply didn't have the temperament for it.

She ran upstairs, retrieved the box of cash in the

diaper bag in the bottom of the closet and stuffed it into her purse.

Then she tiptoed halfway downstairs, stopped to listen to make sure Sal and the baby were still outside, then hurried the rest of the way down and out the front door.

She couldn't start the car, or he would hear her. She glanced at her watch. She had thirty-five minutes to walk to town.

SAL WATCHED Max try to throw his toy and succeed only in dropping it into his lap. It seemed to thrill him, anyway, and he giggled.

This life was a miracle, Sal thought. His marriage with Dori resurrected, this beautiful baby in their lives. He'd feel better about everything when he knew they could keep Max, but they couldn't be sure of that until Brenda Ward was found. And Bram had had no luck so far.

The telephone rang, and Sal picked it up, recognizing Peg and Charlie McKeon's name and number on the small display screen. Knowing Dori would be upset if he answered it, he walked as far as the open kitchen door, his eyes on Max as he listened to the answering machine.

"Hi, Dori," Peg's voice said. "It's Mom. Dad and I just got in from the doctor's, and I wanted to report that he's doing better this week. The doctor was pleased, so thanks for talking to your father so sternly. I think the threat to come and cook for us is what turned him around. Love you. Mom."

Now that was strange, Sal thought. That message

didn't sound as though Peg and Dori had just talked. He went back to the table, pushed the caller ID button and flashed to the call before Peg's.

He frowned as he read the name: Voicestream, and a 555 number. A cell phone. He hit the flash several more times on the chance there'd been a call he hadn't heard. But there hadn't.

He lifted Max out of his playpen and went to the foot of the stairs. "Dori!" he shouted. There was no answer.

An awful suspicion formed in his mind. He ran upstairs and pushed open her office door. The room was empty.

Swearing and hoping Max was too young to pick up bad language, he sprinted out to the front door. He half expected to see the car missing.

Then he realized he would have heard her if she'd started the motor. So that meant she *really* hadn't wanted him to know she was leaving.

He checked the geranium on the porch under which she usually left a spare car key—and found it. He pulled the door closed and ran down the porch steps to the car, fumbling a little as he stuffed Max into his car seat.

Then he ran to the driver's door and let himself in, thinking gratefully that there was only one route to town. And if she'd left on foot, she had only a ten-minute head start on him.

He was sure this had something to do with Brenda Ward. Dori knew he would never let her meet the young woman without him, so she'd put on that performance to keep him out of her way. He didn't know what he was more furious about—the lie or the potential danger in her going off alone.

He spotted her halfway to town, khaki shorts and pink T-shirt swaying in a seductive quick-step as she hurried along, her purse over her shoulder.

Traffic was light, only a log truck far ahead of her and an SUV some distance behind him. He accelerated and reached her just as she turned to cross the highway, probably to walk the rest of the way in the shady shelter of a long line of hawthorne trees.

He pulled up in front of her, just as she stepped off the curb. She looked first startled, then exasperated, then reluctant to get into the car when he leaned across the front seat and opened the door.

"Get in," he ordered quietly.

She seemed to square her shoulders. "I have every—"

"We're not having this argument in the middle of the road," he said. "Get—in."

"If I get in," she asked, remaining stubbornly where she was, "will you just pull over and let me explain?"

He drew a breath for patience. "Your getting in is not negotiable. If I have to get out and put you in the car, neither one of us is going to like it."

She gave him one last defiant look, which he met intrepidly, then climbed in and closed her door. He took the first turnoff to the beach and pulled onto the far end of the pavement where the road met the deep expanse of sand.

He turned off the motor and angled his body in his seat, waiting for her to explain. Max, mercifully, had been mesmerized by the short ride and had fallen asleep.

She glanced at her watch. "Please, Sal," she said urgently. "I have only fifteen minutes left to get there."

He ignored that. "Your mother called," he said. "She and your dad were just back from the doctor's. He's doing well. She credits your threatening to cook with turning him around."

She had the grace to look sheepish.

"So, who called," he asked, "when you told me it was your mother?"

She sighed. "Brenda Ward," she replied, then glanced at her watch. "I have fourteen minutes left." She looked up at him imploringly. "Please let me go."

"Sorry. Where were you meeting her?"

"The park. Sal..."

"Where in the park?"

"The bench behind the playground under the maple tree. Sal..."

He pulled out his cell phone and began to dial.

She reached across him to catch his arm. "Please, don't! I was bringing her the money so she could turn it over to the police. Then she'll sign the release form for me to adopt Max."

He hit the cancel button and started over, giving her a doubtful look.

She caught his arm again. "Sal! If she turns over the money, she might not have to go to jail when they find Valdefiero. But if she finds she *can't* trust me, she might change her mind about Max."

"She let a hoodlum in to steal money from a church!" he reminded her a little hotly. "And you can get Max in court."

"She's trying to right the wrong!"

He shook his head at her. "Or she's trying to lure you there so she can simply get the money back."

"Well, let me find that out for sure!"

After Sal finally dialed the number, Bram Bishop answered. Sal explained the meeting place Dori and Brenda had agreed upon.

Dori slammed back against her seat, tears of temper streaming down her cheeks.

"They were to meet at three o'clock," Sal said. "I'd meet you there, but I don't trust her to go home if I don't take her there myself. So you might want to bring back up. I have a feeling the boyfriend's either involved in it with her, or forced her to set up the meeting. And he was part of a gang, remember, so he might not be there alone."

"I've got it covered," Bram promised. "I'll let you know what happens."

"Thanks."

They drove home in silence. When they arrived, Dori took the baby out of the back of the car, then put him in the crib in the downstairs bedroom and pulled the door partially closed.

Sal went into the kitchen to fill the kettle.

"I thought I'd make tea," he said as she stormed in, "since you only pretended to the last time."

"I am an adult!" she said, so angry that she was on tiptoe as she pointed to herself. "I have every ri—"

"Adults don't lie to one another," he returned calmly, setting the filled kettle on the burner and turning it on.

"Oh, well, that must be why I thought Desideria was your friend and not your sister!"

She had him there, but he wasn't giving an inch on this. He reached above him for cups. "I wasn't the one who introduced you," he reminded her.

"You also never corrected the impression!"

"It was her wish."

"Well, it was Brenda Ward's wish that I meet her at the park!"

He turned to her, hands on his hips, her attitude doing nothing to quiet the temper he was trying very hard to control.

"I can't believe," he pointed out reasonably, "that if you're such an *adult,* it didn't occur to you that meeting her could be dangerous. What if her boyfriend put her up to calling you just to get the money back, and he and his friends were waiting for you at the park, instead of her?"

THAT HADN'T OCCURRED to her until he'd brought it up. It sounded logical when he suggested it, but she simply hadn't thought of it. "She said she wanted to give it to the police," she said stubbornly.

"But she would, wouldn't she? Particularly if she's dealing with someone gullible enough to believe her."

She folded her arms. "Well, it sounded reasonable to me."

"Did it?" he asked pleasantly, leaning back against

the counter. "Then why didn't you tell me where you were going?"

She knew this was a trap, but she answered just to show him she wasn't intimidated. "Because I knew you'd tell me not to go."

"Now, why would I do that?" He watched her innocently, setting her up.

"Because you'd get all paranoid and feel sure it was somehow dangerous."

His temper flashed at her reply, but his voice remained quiet. "And whose instincts would we trust on this? Yours, as a writer and a teacher of English Literature, or mine, as a bodyguard and former thief?"

Her argument lost, she was so frustrated that all she could think to do was turn up the volume. "I just wanted to help her! I know what it's like to have everyone misjudge you!"

"I presume you're talking about the way your family tends to hover over you," he said coolly. "Well after your behavior this afternoon, I don't think you've been misjudged at all. In fact, I don't think it would be out of line to fix you with one of those monitoring anklets."

"Pardon me," she retorted, lowering her voice as she heard the baby stir, "but I don't think you're in a position to judge me, considering you married me, then abandoned me for two years."

He closed his eyes and groaned. "*Dios,* Dori. I think you really having nothing to complain about in your life, so you bring up the old stuff over and over. You're the one who resurrected our marriage by coming to find me, by seducing me, by saving yourself for me. So don't blame *me* because you're too much the baby of the family to know what to do with a real relationship!"

She was so outraged that she sputtered. "I knew what to do with it! You just weren't around to do it with!"

"I'm here now!"

She walked up to within an inch of him and glared up into his face. "Well, I don't need you now. If all you're going to do is tell me what I can and cannot do, then you can get the hell out of my life."

He leaned down to her until they were nose to nose. "Don't lie about it, Dori. You're not upset because you feel overprotected. You're just mad because I stopped you from doing what you wanted to do. I think that's the same problem you have with your brothers. You're just ticked off that you can't do whatever you damn well please. Well, let me tell you, *querida,* it doesn't work that way. Everything you do affects everyone who cares about you. You're not in this alone."

"Well, I'd like to be!" She unscrewed the back of the earring that had once been her wedding ring, and slapped it on the counter. "Hopefully Bram will solve this thing this afternoon, and you can go home. I'll call my lawyer in the morning. I'm going back to work. Call me when Max wakes up, and I'll come down."

She turned with great dignity and walked out of the kitchen, shoulders straight, step resolved. She was only three steps out of the kitchen, when he caught her arm and turned her around.

"You're running away from us again?" he asked, his fingers biting into her arm.

She tried to break free of him, but he held on. "Well, it doesn't seem to be working, does it?"

There was genuine puzzlement in his eyes, as though he couldn't understand why she thought that. "Of course it's working. You just don't want to do what it requires."

"Accede to *your* wishes, you mean?"

"Yes!" he replied hotly. "When that wish is that you don't get yourself hurt, or worse!"

"I've managed for twenty-six years, thank you very much."

He dropped her arm with a resigned expression. "Yes, with an army of McKeons to keep you from harm. Go back to work. Two-hundred-year-old literature seems to be all you have the capacity to understand."

Now no longer concerned with dignity, only escape, Dori hurried up the stairs.

She put Sal out of her mind as she sat stiffly in her chair, trying to remember what she'd been working on when the call had come from Brenda.

Bram called at four forty-five. Dori reached for the phone, but Sal had already picked it up. She ignored it until Sal rapped on her door.

"Bram wants to talk to you," he said, then walked away.

Dori picked up the receiver. "Hi, Bram," she said.

"Dori, hi. I'm sorry, but we weren't able to grab

Brenda. She wasn't on the bench at all, but in a van waiting on the street. I ran the plates, and it's registered to her boyfriend."

Dori hated to believe that strained voice hadn't been genuine. "He probably forced her to call me."

"That's possible," Bram said. "But had you gone, the result would have been the same whether he forced her or she did it on her own. He was there with several friends."

"Thank you, Bram."

"Sure. I'll be in touch."

She hung up the phone and went downstairs. She found Sal in the kitchen. The aroma of chili wafted out of a big pot on a back burner, and the room was filled with the smell of baking cornbread.

He usually cut up jalapénos in it, she remembered absently.

Max sat in the high chair with a handful of Cheerios. Dori went to him when he uttered a shrill sound and reached for her. She lifted him onto her hip, loving the way he bounced in her arms, clearly happy to see her.

Sal turned from chopping green onions, probably for the salad in a bowl on the counter.

"The boyfriend was there," Dori said.

Sal nodded. "Bram told me."

"So you were right and I was wrong." She knew her tone was not at all conciliatory.

He nodded again. "The world will not collapse."

"But it doesn't change anything," she insisted stiffly. "I'm calling my lawyer in the morning."

"So you've said."

"We've always been a mistake."

He shrugged a shoulder. "So it would seem."

Dori was a little startled to hear him admit that. He'd always been so insistent that it would work out, if she would simply listen, or change, or something.

It seemed to burn a little hole inside her. It must really be over if he thought so, too.

Suddenly her brain was filled with memories of the past several days, of their happiness together and their delight in Max's tiny bud of a tooth, in his ability to sit up, memories of the lovemaking that made her forget everything for a time, except how perfectly she and Sal fit together, and how wonderful she felt in his arms.

She made herself nod amiably. "Well. This should be easier to deal with now that we're in agreement."

He turned back to the chili. "We can only hope. Are you ready for dinner?"

"Are you ready to serve?"

He grinned at her over his shoulder as he checked the cornbread. "Don't be too agreeable. Then the world might collapse, after all."

She listened to the local radio station while preparing for bed that night, and heard the pastor of Faith Community profusely thank the anonymous donor who'd replaced the stolen roof-fund money.

"Our entire congregation will pray for you," he promised. "Whoever you are."

Feeling oddly defeated, Dori got into bed. How did a woman stand up against the man who'd just earned the prayers of hundreds of God-fearing people?

CHAPTER TEN

DORI STUMBLED DOWN to breakfast at seven. Max, riding her hip, was far too lively for a baby who'd been up most of the night teething. The companion tooth to his first was breaking through, and he'd been up every hour on the hour. Or so it had felt.

Sal had offered to relieve her twice, but she'd turned him down politely, determined that she was going to learn to function without the man coming to her aid all the time.

But she hadn't expected to have to do it without breakfast. The table was set with silverware, and a nice aroma lingered, but the kitchen was quiet.

Sal's bedroom door had been open when she'd passed, and she'd seen that his bed was made. Had he left already, she wondered? Had he decided not to wait until the issue of Brenda and her boyfriend was resolved?

She had a brief mental image of that face in the window the other night, of her planned meeting with Brenda's boyfriend yesterday—which hadn't happened but might have—and realized for the first time what it would have felt like to be alone through all of that.

Was she about to face the rest of it alone? As fear

threatened to overwhelm her, she reminded herself that this was what she wanted. She could do this. At the moment she didn't particularly want to, but she could.

The back door was open, summer fragrances wafting through on a breeze. She went to the screen door and looked out. There was no one at the picnic table, and only Cheddar occupied the hammock.

Everything inside Dori seemed to sink to her toes.

"I guess it's just you and me, baby," she said to Max, putting him in his high chair and going to the cupboard for more Cheerios to keep him happy until she could mix baby cereal.

There was an odd pressure in her heart and in her throat. But she'd be fine. Fine.

She put a bright yellow plastic bowl with the Cheerios on Max's tray, then went to the refrigerator for the carton of eggs and the gallon of milk.

When she turned around to bump the door closed with her hip, a man stood there, startling her out of her wits. She managed to juggle the egg carton, but the milk fell like a stone. The wax container exploded, and milk flew everywhere.

Max, apparently of the opinion that she'd done it just for his entertainment, laughed gleefully.

Sal, momentarily unfamiliar in a white T-shirt and jeans, arched an eyebrow at her violent reaction.

She closed her eyes as her pulse dribbled back to normal. When she opened them again, she saw that the basket he held contained black cherries, half a dozen navel oranges, several fat, glossy plums, and a bunch of green grapes. The spray of milk had fortunately been close to the ground and had missed her shorts and his jeans.

"Sorry," he said. "Mrs. Fisher up the hill came over with these. She and her husband are just back from a cruise, and bought these at a roadside stand yesterday on their way home from Portland."

Once Dori got over her alarm, a sense of relief and renewed security filled her, despite the milk mess. But she tried to act casual.

"*I'm* sorry," she said. "I got very little sleep."

He nodded, stepping carefully over the little white river to put the basket on the counter. "I heard you. I'll get the mop."

"I'll clean it up." She, too, moved cautiously to put the eggs on the counter. "It's my mess."

She stopped arguing when she heard him fill a bucket in the service porch. She got a colander from a bottom cupboard and put the fruit in it to rinse.

"I'll start breakfast," she said, as Sal reappeared with the sudsy bucket and a sponge mop.

He frowned at her as he set to work. "I've eaten. Your breakfast is in the oven."

"It is?" She peered in, surprised, and found a plate of golden-brown French toast and a pipkin of syrup warming. No wonder the kitchen was aromatic. She reached for a pot holder and pulled them out. "Thank you."

"Sure," he said as he worked. "I presume that part of the deal remains in effect? I cook while you work?"

Before she could answer, there was a firm, even authoritative knock on the front door. Hoping that didn't mean her brothers were home early, Dori went to answer it.

"Wait!" Sal shouted.

An impatient retort came to her lips, but she bit it back and spread her arms in an exaggerated gesture, ushering him before her.

"Stay in here with the baby," he said. "Eat your breakfast."

She rolled her eyes. "You know, one day you're going to need me to defend *you,* only you won't call for me because it won't occur to you that I'm competent enough to help."

He'd started toward the door, then turned back to her, apparently surprised by her remark. "How have you gotten that so twisted?" he asked.

Now she was surprised. "What?"

"The concept of man and woman," he replied, as another series of loud raps sounded on the door. "We protect you not because you're incapable, but because you're precious to us."

He strode toward the door, and she remained where she stood, made boneless by that explanation.

Sal opened the door.

Dori couldn't see beyond him, but she didn't have to. She recognized the gasp instantly, and the shrieked "Sal! Oh, my God, it's true! I can't believe it!"

Her mother. Dori put both hands to her face and thought that if anything could worsen a morning that had started with a sleepless night and spilled milk, it was the arrival of Peg McKeon.

"Peg. How nice to see you." Sal leaned down for her mother's hug, then drew her into the house. He turned to Dori with a bland look that she interpreted as barely concealed delight over her impending doom. "Dori, your mom's here."

Dori came forward to hug her mother. Meetings among the McKeons after a separation of more than a day always began with a hug, whether the purpose of the meeting was friendly or hostile.

Her mother returned the hug, then stepped back to shake her finger at her. Peg's eyebrows converged, her cheeks pinked and her mouth had a definite downward curve.

"Dorianne Margaret McKeon!" she said as though Dori were four years old. "You are in so much trouble!"

Tell me about it, Dori thought. This confrontation with her mother was probably going to be worse than anything Brenda's boyfriend could have conceived.

"Would you like some coffee, Peg?" Sal asked, leading her to the sofa. "A cup of tea?"

"I'll have two fingers of brandy," Peg replied, settling into the middle of the sofa, her arms crossed over the purse in her lap. "And please don't dawdle. Charlie and Dori's aunt Letitia and cousin Natalie are on their way. Well, they're not on their way, they're waiting for me to get back to the restaurant, but they'll *be* here today—and we have to clear up a few things before they arrive."

That didn't entirely make sense to Dori, but she felt a very lively sense of panic, anyway. For a woman who was created from the same gene pool as Dori's father, Aunt Titia had none of his endearing qualities. She was pushy, condescending and forever putting her children forward as superior to her brother's—something that had always entertained the McKeon boys because they'd all been overachievers and hadn't cared. Dori had laughed, too, because it was expected of her.

Gordon Browning was a physicist, and Chase Browning had something to do with software at the Pentagon. Dori hadn't cared much about the successes of her male cousins. No one really compared her to them. But Nattie was an anchor on the KRTV Philadelphia evening news. Natalie was five foot nine, golden blond, with wide gray eyes and delicate features in a face that was a perfect oval.

"How is little Dori?" Aunt Titia would usually preface an interrogation. "She must have a boyfriend by now! Does she have that degree yet? Has she started on *the book?*" Titia always verbally italicized *the book*. When the book was finished, Titia was definitely one of the people Dori intended to invite to her autograph party.

"What is she doing here?" Dori asked now, sitting in a corner of the sofa, reminding herself that this summer was about taking control. It's a shame it wasn't about telling lies and springing surprises, she thought in a state of mild hysteria. She'd have that one sewn up.

Peg waved a hand dismissively. "I don't know. Nattie's getting some honor or other in San Francisco, and Titia's riding her coattails. But that's not what I'm here to talk about!"

Dori accepted that with a nod. "What are you here to talk about?"

Peg yanked her purse open and removed a copy of the local newspaper, folded in four. Dori knew her mother and father subscribed to the paper and had it mailed to their home in Edenfield so they could keep abreast of Dancer's Beach happenings.

"I was reading this last night, when your aunt called from the Portland airport and said she and Nattie were on their way to San Francisco and thought it would be nice if they dropped in on the relatives on their way."

Her mother made a face and added as a personal aside, "You know. Spread a little cheer among the peasants. Let them see how the other half lives. The only one of you children she's ever had any respect for is Duncan because he's a big star, but she told me just last night that he'll finally get somewhere when he gets a television series. It made me want to put her head in the microwave on defrost at the first opportunity!"

The image almost made Dori smile, but she was pretty sure that wasn't the right move at the moment. So she just listened.

"'Nattie would love to see her cousin,'" Peg quoted Letitia. "Of course, I interpreted that to mean that Nattie wanted to come and gloat that she has a three-carat diamond, and that little Dori is still single and living alone in a beach house writing a book."

"I'm—" Dori attempted to interrupt but was turned off with a dark look.

"So, I promised we'd come. They can only stay one night because they have to be in San Francisco the day after tomorrow. Well, your father's going stir-crazy in the house, so I thought, wouldn't it be nice if we all paid a surprise visit to Dori? So we pile in the car early this morning, and I'm telling them that you now have your degree and you *are* working on the book, and Nattie says we should plan to take you out to lunch since you probably won't want to cook—at which point Titia reminds everyone of the potato salad incident at the family reunion..."

"I explained," Dori said with a sigh, amazed that Aunt Titia still remembered, "that lots of people have made the sugar and salt mistake."

"I know, and we all understand because we love you—but we're talking about your aunt Titia."

"So, to continue...?"

"Right. Well. Because I'm driving, I ask your father to look in the paper, which I've brought along because there was a coupon in it for twenty-percent off anything at the antique shop, and I wanted to check to see if Burgers by the Sea has anything but burgers. I know you kids go there all the time, but your father and I usually eat at home when we're here."

She accepted a jigger of brandy from Sal, took a swig Dori was sure would cause her to turn purple, then continued with barely a grimace. "Then your father says, 'Peg, let's stop at Burgers and see for ourselves what's on the lunch menu.'" I look at him to tell him we can just call from your house, and he's wearing this odd, desperate look. You know your father. He doesn't know how to panic."

Dori nodded. Everyone knew that.

"He insisted we stop for coffee and check it out.

Your aunt said she was tired and needed a bathroom, and why didn't we go straight to Dori's, but Nattie said it'd be a good idea to check it out and she could use a cup of coffee. So we stopped." Peg drew another breath, took another deep swig, then shook the paper to unfold it. "And while Titia and Nattie are in the bathroom, your father shows me *this!*"

She handed the paper over. Sal leaned over the back of the sofa to read over Dori's shoulder. It was the editorial page, where Burgers by the Sea always had an ad.

And then she saw the column entitled "On the Public Record." The third item was about the prowler at the beach house, and all the information was correct—including the names of the residents with whom the police had spoken: Salvatore Dominguez and Dorianne Dominguez.

"So, on the pretext of not being able to reach you by phone to tell you we were coming," her mother said, "I left them at the restaurant and came to see if you were home while they're relaxing with coffee."

It was a plot worthy of the CIA, Dori thought.

"Dominguez?" her mother asked, her voice rising an octave and a decibel. She finished the brandy. "Dorianne *Dominguez?*"

Dori folded the paper and handed it back. "We were married," she said, knowing she was going to have to be firm if she was going to take control of this situation, "in Mexico."

"What?" Peg demanded. "When did you go to Mexico?"

Dori enjoyed her mother's shock. Peg was usually

so unshockable. And then Dori remembered that she had to tell her how long ago it had been.

"Two years ago," she replied with a matter-of-factness that was completely bogus. "I'd just come back from England and I'd been thinking about him all the time and I decided that maybe I was wrong about us and that I should see if he still felt the same."

Her mother looked up at Sal. "And you did?"

"I did," he replied.

"Well, pardon me for wanting to murder both of you!" Peg shouted. "But why wasn't her family invited to the wedding?"

Dori opened her mouth to reply, but Sal cut her off with "I take responsibility for that." He looked properly penitent. "I insisted that we get married right away. I didn't know what had changed her mind, or what might change it back, so we were married within a week of her arrival in Madre Maria."

Peg looked from one to the other in astonishment. "And you've been married for two whole years, and no one told us? How can that be?"

Dori sighed. This was going to be grizzly. "Because we've been married for two years but we haven't lived together since our wedding day."

Peg picked up the jigger, now empty of brandy, and looked as though she might chew the glass. "Why?"

Dori explained.

Peg frowned at Sal. Dori waited for her to lay into him for leaving her daughter on their wedding day, but all she said was "I can't believe we weren't invited."

"I'm sorry," he said.

Then there was a loud, prolonged shout from the kitchen and the banging of little feet against the high chair's footboard.

Peg lifted her chin, and Dori knew she was scenting the air, like a predator that had found new prey. "What is that?"

Dori put both hands over her eyes.

"I'll show you," Sal said, and disappeared into the kitchen.

Dori concluded later that Max was the only reason her mother didn't kill them both. Sal put him in Peg's lap and she was transformed instantly from an angry goddess to a besotted earth mother. Max responded brilliantly to her effusive attention.

"So, he was conceived in that week before your wedding day?" her mother considered. "We can pass that off to Aunt Titia as a wedding-night home run."

Sal now sat in a chair opposite the sofa and met Dori's eyes. His gaze said she had to take responsibility for this one.

"Mom, Max was left in my car," Dori began. At her mother's shocked expression, she explained about finding the baby, about going to Sal, about his insistence on returning with her. But she left out the face at the window and the aborted meeting with Brenda.

Peg dandled the baby on her knee and made funny faces at him, while he watched in fascination. "Sal," she said, her tone of voice not at all in line with her comic expressions. "Are you telling me you're here only to keep them safe until this mystery is solved?"

Dori suddenly saw a way to redeem herself. "Actually," Dori said, willing him with her eyes to understand her course of action and follow it, "we've fallen in love again since we've been here together."

"You have?" Peg glanced away from the baby to catch Sal's eye. Hers were hopeful.

He was still staring at Dori, his expression telling her she couldn't throw him out of her life one minute and expect him to act the lover the next.

She pleaded with a look. "Haven't we, *querido?*"

SAL ENJOYED THE MOMENT. She was wheedling—and charming about it—but he had to have more than that.

He looked away from her to smile at her mother. "Spending time with your daughter is always an experience."

Peg rolled her eyes. "I raised her. I know that. But do you love her, after what she's done to you?"

Dori gasped. "What *I've* done to *him?*" she demanded. "He left me on—!"

"Your wedding day," her mother nodded. "The same thing your brothers would have done for you had *your* life been in danger. And don't forget that he saved you from Suarez."

Dori fell back against the sofa with a groan. "Mother, I—"

Peg didn't even hear her. "I want to hear you tell me that you love her," she insisted to Sal.

Well. That was true enough. "Yes, I do love her," he said.

Peg hugged the baby to her and nibbled on his neck. He laughed in hysterical little hiccups. "Thank God! Then we can bring Titia and Nattie here, and everything will be fine!" She waggled her eyebrows greedily. "And my daughter's married before hers to a handsome man in a sexy and dangerous business. Oh, this is almost too good! And a baby to boot! Nattie's going to be so jealous of you!"

Dori almost felt sorry for her cousin. They'd always liked each other well enough, but though Nattie had never precisely bragged, she'd been happy to list each new accomplishment at family gatherings. Dori had been delighted when the Brownings moved to the east coast when Nattie was in high school. They'd seen each other only occasionally since then.

"Okay! Sal, come and take this baby so I can get back to the restaurant and report that you're home and eager to see us."

Dori saw her mother to the door, then returned at a run, picking up toys and fluffing and redistributing pillows.

"DID MAX EVER have anything but those Cheerios?" Sal asked her, keeping his voice and his manner deliberately polite.

"Uh, no." She dropped the toys into a laundry basket she kept in a corner.

"Okay." He carried Max back into the kitchen, put him in his high chair, and found the baby cereal and the bowl Dori had taken down for breakfast. He mixed the cereal up while Max protested the delay.

Then Sal sat beside him and concentrated on spooning in one bite after another.

Dori flew into the kitchen a few minutes later with teacups she tended to hoard upstairs. She put them into the dishwasher and chewed on one of her now cold pieces of French toast while she added other things to the rack. After she closed the washer, she poured out the last half cup of coffee in the carafe and made another pot.

"What'll we do for dinner?" she asked anxiously, wiping off the counters. "When did you finish mopping up the milk?"

"When I got your mother's brandy. And don't worry about dinner. I'll make cheese enchiladas, rice, beans and salad."

She looked doubtful. "This is my aunt Titia. She hates everything."

"Then it doesn't matter what we prepare, does it?"

She came to sit in the chair on the other side of the baby so she could look at him. Her eyes were dark with worry and uncertainty. She tried to smile. "Thank you for saying you love me. Otherwise, my mother really would have freaked."

He didn't look at her, but spooned baby cereal into Max's open mouth. Max kicked and banged his hands on the tray, clearly enjoying it.

"I didn't do that for you," he informed her.

She looked momentarily upset. "Then why did you do it?"

Max reached for the next bite, but Sal held firmly to the spoon. "Because it was true," he replied, holding the baby's free hand down. "But she doesn't have to know that between us love isn't everything."

She looked as though she wanted to argue, but she knew there wasn't time. Still, there was obviously something else on her mind.

"What?" he asked. When Max started to wrestle him for the spoon, he gave it to him and capped the baby food jar.

"I just want to...to make sure..." She was having trouble getting out whatever it was. He didn't feel inclined to help her.

"To make sure," she repeated, "that you—you know—sort of...*act* like you love me."

She heaved a sigh once that was out.

He put the baby food jar in the refrigerator, then wet a paper towel and dabbed at the baby's face. The action required the speed of a quick-draw artist.

"You intend to choreograph the action?" he asked, untying the messy bib.

She sounded offended. "No. So that I won't be humiliated in front of my aunt and my cousin. Having a handsome, sexy, dangerous husband who could care less about me would be worse than being single and all by myself, working on my book."

He met her eyes. "And why does what she thinks matter?" he asked.

She shrugged. "Because Nattie's always been better at everything than me. Because everybody's always known she's special, and I've just been 'little' Dori, who always had her nose in a book when everyone else was doing something big."

He shook his head at her. "I think you wish you

were different, more than your family wishes you were different. I don't think they compare you with the boys or your cousins—I think *you* do. And for reasons I don't understand—unless you consider how bad you are at being in love—you don't think you rate well by comparison."

She looked desperate. The subject was a little heavy for the ticking clock.

"Just tell me," she pleaded, "that you'll act like a loving husband."

"What's in it for me?" he asked brutally.

She played with her fingers. "What do you want?"

"You'll have to sleep with me tonight," he said, "if you want me to look like a loving husband."

"I know. I've thought about that."

"Well, I've spent enough nights in the same bed with you without touching you. I want to make love to you."

She looked troubled. He couldn't decide whether she found the idea distasteful or simply surprising. "All right," she finally replied.

"Then you've got a deal." He offered his hand across the table.

She reached over to shake it. Then she sighed dispiritedly. "I hope it works better than the last deal we made."

"The promise to love each other until death do us part?" he asked. "Or the one we made on the way over *not* to love each other?"

She stood and spread her arms helplessly. "We haven't successfully completed either one.

"Yes, we have. The only problem is, you kept one promise and I kept the other."

CHAPTER ELEVEN

DORI'S AUNT TITIA was tall and angular and very elegantly dressed. She wore pants and a loose shirt in a silky gray fabric that billowed out behind her as she moved, a little like royal robes.

She had side-parted, chin-length gray hair that curved around the strong bones of her face in a flattering frame. A wave at her left temple was streaked with white.

She was perfectly put together, Sal thought, but without the spark of warmth and humor that made beauty live.

Her daughter Natalie had it, he noticed. She was as tall as her mother and slender, but more shapely than angular. She wore the large diamond Dori had talked about, but there was a sweetness in her smile that couldn't be manufactured.

"Well, there's little Dori," Titia said, gathering her niece into her embrace. Dori became lost in the woman's height and voluminous shirt. "How are you, darling?" she enquired in the tone of voice with which someone might ask *Did anyone come out alive?*

Natalie rolled her eyes in an expression of amused sympathy. Then she hugged Dori herself.

"Hey, Dori!" she said, holding her cousin away to look at her. "I love your hair! I've always been so jealous that you have that great brain, yet you'll always look sixteen. It isn't fair, you know."

"Yeah, right." Dori laughed. "You're such a mud fence with only two million viewers every day."

Sal, with Max on his hip, moved up behind Dori.

Titia turned from a smiling perusal of her daughter and her niece, and noticed Sal for the first time. Her eyes went from him to the baby to Dori, then back again in growing puzzlement.

"Titia, I'd like you to meet my son-in-law," Peg said with obvious relish, "Salvatore Dominguez. Sal, this is Charlie's sister, Letitia Browning."

Sal shook Titia's hand. She stared at him and said nothing.

"And this is our niece, Natalie. Nattie, meet Sal."

Natalie smiled warmly at him and gave him a quick hug. "Well, how wonderful! I don't mean to be rude, Sal, but you don't look like someone she met in a library."

"He's the one who kidnapped her at the airport during the Julie incident," Peg said, clearly enjoying herself. "Remember, we talked about it on the phone the Christmas after it happened and you said it sounded so romantic? Well, apparently it was. Sal now has a security firm in Seattle."

"My goodness." Natalie sighed. "Well, now I'm even more jealous than ever. A husband who looks like a mature Ricky Martin, and a baby?"

"The baby, Max, is going to be theirs eventually, but that's rather a long story. Why don't we all get comfortable, first?" Peg prepared to shoo everyone into the living room, but a frowning Titia stopped her with a "Well!"

"Mom," Sal heard Natalie warn her mother under her breath.

"I don't remember hearing about a wedding," Titia insisted. "And I do not remember receiving an invitation."

"We were married in Mexico," Dori said. "Kind of quickly. My parents didn't even know until... later."

Titia looked Sal over again. "Mexico? I suppose your family's there?"

Sal put a hand on Dori's shoulder and drew her just a little closer. "No. They're gone. This is my family."

Natalie held her hands out to Max, who leaned toward her, showing his obvious good taste. She took him into her arms and sat with him in a chair.

Titia frowned. "Well, what ever happened to big family weddings where everyone was invited? Chase and his fiancée tried to pull one of those elopement things on me, and I said, 'Absolutely not!' Why not tell the world you're getting married, unless you have something to hide?"

"You mean, like our criminal pasts?" Dori asked her aunt seriously.

Sal was happy to leap into the middle. "Or the two children we had out of wedlock?"

Peg's eyes widened. Charlie turned away with a cough and limped toward the sofa.

Titia blinked. "I wasn't suggesting..." she began, her voice a little high.

"Good," Sal said, "because we weren't hiding anything." He wrapped his arm around Dori's shoulders and pulled her against his body. "We're just very independent people who knew we wanted to be together. We just couldn't decide on whose terms. So when she came to visit me in Mexico, I didn't want her to have a chance to change her mind. So I married her as quickly as I could."

Titia blinked again. "I see."

"He's a man of action, Mom," Natalie said from the chair, where she lifted the giggling baby up and down and laughed at his delight. "You just haven't known any of those. Come and sit down."

Titia frowned at Peg. "You were going to explain about the baby."

"Yes." Peg led her to the sofa. "Get comfortable. It's an interesting story."

"I'll get us something cold to drink." Dori slipped out of Sal's arm and went into the kitchen.

"Charlie, if you give me your keys," Sal said, "I'll get your bags out of the car and take them upstairs."

Charlie struggled off the sofa, as the women began to talk. "I'll give you a hand."

Sal started to tell him that wasn't necessary, thinking of his new knee, but Charlie gave him a look that told him they had things to talk about.

Once outside, Charlie didn't pull any punches. "You married my baby without telling me," he accused.

"Yes, I did," Sal admitted, as he walked and Charlie hobbled to the van.

"I got a very garbled account of what happened from Peg after she put Titia and Natalie in the van and got me aside on the pretext of making reservations for lunch at Burgers by the Sea. Reservations! At Burgers! Do you see the level of subterfuge she's sunk to!"

Sal found all of that more comic than upsetting, but then, he didn't have to live with Peg.

"I'm sorry," he said again.

"I don't want you to be sorry," Charlie said querulously. "What's done is done, and I always liked you. But from what I got from Peg in a shouted whisper behind the Dumpster at Burgers, you two quarreled again the day of the wedding and have been separated all this time and just got together again because of the baby—" Charlie winced "—that was left in her car?"

"That's right?"

"My God."

"I know."

"And you've fallen in love again?"

He didn't want to lie to Charlie, but found a way to tell him the truth. "I never fell *out* of love with her. She's just stubborn and hardheaded and wouldn't listen to reason."

Charlie laughed mirthlessly. "We all know where that comes from."

"Her mother and some throwback to her aunt Titia?" Sal guessed.

Charlie smiled, his mood lightening. "You got that

right. I just want some reassurance that you're making her happy.''

Again, the truth just had to be carefully put. "When she lets me, I make her happy."

Charlie sighed. "And does she make *you* happy?"

Sal thought that through and finally sighed. "She makes me crazy," he replied candidly. "She makes me question everything I know to be true, including my own sanity. She doesn't do anything the way I would or see anything the way I see it. Sometimes she makes me feel as though I'm speaking Martian. But somehow she reaches me here—" He put a hand over his heart. "She bypasses my brain altogether, but I feel as though my heart doesn't beat without her."

Charlie patted his shoulder sympathetically. "You poor devil. If it's any comfort, it evens out a little as you mature, but you're never going to belong to yourself again, and the world will always be a little off-kilter."

Sal nodded, accepting that. "Thank God for gravity."

Charlie laughed. "And whiskey."

DORI INSISTED on helping Sal with dinner. He wore a white apron over a black shirt and pants, and grinned at her over the steam rising from sauteeing onions.

"Have you suddenly learned to cook?" he asked.

"Ha, ha," she said, refusing to take offense. Then she added softly, "I just think it'll look better if I'm helping."

"Won't it 'look better' if you're out there entertaining your aunt?"

She shuddered dramatically. "Please don't make me go back out there."

"Your choice. Want to make the salad?"

"Sure." She was capable of washing lettuce and chopping vegetables. She pulled the greens and other makings out of the crisper. "Ah, lettuce in a bag," she said, finding the scissors to cut it open. "I'd be such a happy camper if you could buy stuffed pork chops in a bag, or chicken Kiev."

"You can probably find those things frozen."

"I know, but that's not the same."

"Then you have to move to the big city where you can be closer to a good delicatessen."

She emptied the lettuce into a large stainless steel bowl, then dropped radishes, green onions, red and yellow peppers, and tomatoes into a colander and rinsed them.

"I was just beginning to think I might move here full time," she said, smiling in his direction to show that she had no hard feelings about what had happened. She would have loved to live in that old house behind the Bijou.

"This place does grow on you," he said, adding chopped garlic to the pan.

"But you like the big city." She dried off vegetables with paper towels and put the green onions on a cutting board.

"I do. And it would be difficult to find enough clients to sustain a security firm in Dancer's Beach."

"So, what would you do if you had to decide upon a second career?"

He smiled. "It would be a third career. I was a thief first, remember?"

She stopped chopping onions to frown at him. "Why do you keep bringing that up? Do you miss the life, or wish you could erase it from your past?"

His smile waned just a little, and he turned back to add tomato puree, bouillon, and other herbs and spices to the pan. "I guess since we've had Max around, I've been thinking that it's not a very good thing for a child to have a father who was a thief."

"He'd have a father," she reminded him, "who helped his family support a village that otherwise wouldn't even have had basic education and health services."

"I think we need some juice," Natalie said, walking into the kitchen with a wailing Max. "Or milk, or something. I've been doing pretty well with him all afternoon, but either he's decided that I'm not the woman he wanted, after all, or he's hungry."

Dori laughed. "Guys react pretty much the same way to either problem. Here, I'll take him."

"No, you look busy. I can give him a bottle, if that's what he wants."

Dori got one out of the refrigerator and ran it under the hot water. "Maybe if we're lucky, he'll go to sleep with this, and we'll have a peaceful dinner. Do you need something to munch on until then?"

Natalie shook her head. "I'm still stuffed from our burgers at lunch."

Dori handed her the bottle, then a clean tea towel

to put over her shoulder. "Now that he's getting teeth, he's droolly. Does your fiancée like children?"

Natalie frowned. "Actually, we've been arguing about that. When we first got engaged, he was just a bit actor on a soap. Now he's on the short list for the starring role in a new sitcom that's going to film in Malibu. He's saying we have to put off the baby because he'll have too much to worry about."

She sounded troubled, and Dori felt sorry for her. When they were young, they played dolls together all the time. Natalie had always wanted babies as much as Dori had.

"Well, how do you feel about it?"

Max had already helped himself to the bottle, and Natalie settled him in the crook of her arm. She made a face. "I don't think it would be wise to coerce someone who doesn't want a baby into having one."

"Sounds to me," Sal contributed, "as though you need to put off the fiancé, not the baby."

Natalie turned to him, new interest in her eyes. "I thought most men were eager to avoid the responsibility of children."

He shook his head. "Not the ones I know."

"Or forget the fiancé altogether," Dori said, "and have the baby without him."

"Without him?"

"Sperm banks are one way to go if you want a baby but don't necessarily want to deal with a man."

"Hmm." Natalie smiled over that. "Now, there's something to think about. This guy's getting heavy. I'm going to go sit down."

"I like her," Sal said, as Natalie walked into the

living room. "She's very elegant. And there has to be the right man for her somewhere."

"I know," Dori said mournfully. "I've always wanted to look like her. Then I wouldn't be 'little' Dori."

He laughed lightly. "No, you'll always be 'little' Dori because you're small and petite, and because you always look a little lost, as though you're not sure where you belong. So there's a tendency to think of you as someone who needs protection."

"Great." She chopped vigorously. "It isn't likely that I'll grow any more, or that I can change my facial expression, so I'll probably be 'little' Dori forever."

"Enjoy it," he advised. "I'll bet there are lots of people who'd love to have someone worry about them."

Everyone enjoyed Sal's enchiladas. Dori watched her aunt try to needle him, but he remained resolutely polite and charming.

"I can't believe you kept a baby that you found in the back of your car!" she said, turning to Dori when she couldn't upset Sal.

"I didn't want to turn him in to the police," Dori said calmly. "I just fell in love with him."

"We have a detective looking for his mother," Sal added. "When we find her, we can formally file for adoption."

"I don't understand why you just don't have your own."

"We'll do that, too."

Titia shook her head. "You don't tell anyone

you're married, you keep a baby that isn't even yours. I don't understand this generation."

"Love makes him theirs, Mom," Natalie said. "And the wedding was their business. Family is wonderful, but sometimes you just have to do what you have to do."

Titia turned on her suspiciously. "If you got married and didn't tell me, I'd never forgive you."

"Then, I guess I'd have to live with that," Natalie said.

Titia turned to Peg and Charlie in horror. "I can't believe what this generation is coming to."

Sal calmed the atmosphere by serving flan for dessert. The conversation turned to the accomplishments of Titia's two sons, and everyone listened dutifully. It was after nine when she pleaded weariness and excused herself to retire for the night.

"Thank you for a wonderful dinner," she said politely to Sal. "I don't understand why little Dori married you without inviting her parents and her family, but I do understand *why* she married you."

Sal bowed modestly. "I appreciate that. Thank you."

When Titia's back was turned on her way to the stairs, Peg gave Sal a thumbs-up.

"Sal and I have been using your bedroom," Dori explained to her parents, "because it was more convenient with the baby. You'd probably like to sleep upstairs tonight, because he's up a couple of times a night. You'll get a better night's sleep."

Peg nodded. "Whatever's more convenient."

"But can your father do the stairs?" Sal asked.

Charlie nodded. "I'm supposed to work out a little on them, so that'll be fine." He asked with an interested twinkle, "What's for breakfast? We have to be at the Portland airport by eleven a.m."

Peg backhanded him in his paunchy stomach. "Cereal and fruit. You ate enough tonight to put your cholesterol in four figures."

Sal leaned toward him conspiratorially. "I'll see what I can do for you," he whispered.

Dori wasn't sure why it pleased her that her father liked Sal—and that Sal liked her father. She would have to call her parents when they got home from the airport tomorrow afternoon and explain that her story about the rebirth of their marriage had been for the benefit of Aunt Titia—and that she was getting a divorce.

But Dori enjoyed watching her mother hug him good-night. And Dori liked the sparkle in Peg's eyes when she smiled up at Sal and told him how much she'd enjoyed dinner and how valuable an addition he was to the family, with his suave good manners and his cooking skills.

She also enjoyed the new respect in her mother's eyes when she hugged Dori good-night.

"I'm upset that you didn't tell us you were married all this time," Peg scolded gently. "But I do applaud you on your good taste and your good sense. I don't think your father and I could have done a better job of finding a man for you than you did yourself. Congratulations."

That was high praise, indeed. She basked in the glory of it, while Sal helped her father upstairs. Natalie loaded the dishwasher, while Dori wiped off counters and filled the coffeepot for the following morning.

"Now, I'm more jealous than ever," Natalie said, redistributing cups to make room for one more.

"He is a great cook," Dori said.

Natalie nodded. "He is, but I'm not talking about that. I'm talking about the way he looks at you and touches you. As though you'll never have anything to fear again."

Dori made a face. "Because I'm 'little' Dori."

Natalie frowned over that. "No. It's more than just protective, it's...possessive. That's what I'd like to see in a man's eyes, but the twenty-first century really doesn't allow for that—unless you're lucky enough to find a man raised with Old World ways. And he looks at the baby the same way, even though Max isn't his biologically."

Dori pushed the filter basket in place and filled the water well with filtered water. "Your fiancé..."

"Is wonderful in many ways." Natalie pushed the dishwasher door closed, then studied the controls. "Shall I leave it the way it's set?" At Dori's nod, she started it, and they moved by mutual consent to the table and sat down.

"It's just that he's a very contemporary man. I loved that, at first. My work is all very immediate and I thought I was, too. Until he told me we had to put off having a baby. Then I began to have very old-fashioned feelings about motherhood and home and hearth." She smiled across the table at Dori—a smile of congratulations.

"We're all trying so hard to be in the game, you know what I mean? To show how sophisticated and independent we are. And I wonder if we aren't completely losing the ability to live for each other—to know how to love wholeheartedly."

She leaned her chin on her hand and laughed at herself. "Listen to me. I don't know what's gotten into me lately. I've always been fairly self-confident and comfortable with who I am, but suddenly I'm questioning everything. I'm wondering if it isn't nature's way of telling me that I'm on the wrong road or something. That I should stop and think before I take another step."

Dori nodded. "Stopping to think would never be a bad move, would it?"

"No, I don't think so." Natalie straightened in her chair and heaved a sigh, as though she'd come to a decision. "And now that I've seen what you have, I want that, too." She laughed again. "Sal's yours, I know. But I want someone like him. Someone who looks at me as though I'm his everything."

She reached across the table to cover Dori's hands with her own. "I'm so glad I got to see you. I remember what fun we used to have as little girls, before my mother's competitive syndrome took over my life."

Dori turned her hands to squeeze Natalie's. "I think you should go for whatever it is you want. Maybe there's something in the air, because that was my plan for the summer, too. I wanted to gain my independence and write my book."

"Is it working?"

"I'm not sure." Dori grinned wryly. "It's hard to assert your independence when your life is filled with a demanding baby and a...a possessive man."

"Yeah, well right now I'd kill for either of those. Preferably both." Natalie stood and hugged Dori. "Thanks for your hospitality. We'll have to keep in better touch. You must have an e-mail address?"

"I do." Dori retrieved a business card from her daytimer on the edge of the counter.

Natalie looked at it as though it were precious. "My cards are upstairs. I'll leave one with you in the morning." She hugged her again. "You love that man—and fight for that baby."

"I will," Dori promised. "Good night."

As Natalie went upstairs, Dori stood alone in the middle of the kitchen, feeling as though her entire world was off balance, slipping on its axis, spinning out of control.

Possession meant ownership. How could that be a good thing?

Not that Sal treated her in any way like a slave or a piece of property. However, he did seem to feel entitled to affect or even change some of her decisions, usually in what he considered her best interest. That resulted in her losing control, didn't it?

She heard Sal's footsteps on the stairs; then he walked into the kitchen, unrolling the sleeves he'd folded back while cooking.

"Your parents are settled," he said, his eyes going over her face. "Is something troubling you? I thought the evening went well. We all managed to blockade your aunt so that she couldn't ruin things."

She had to agree. And looking into his face when night had fallen and the house was still always made her wonder why she worried about their relationship in the first place. His quiet, intelligent eyes watching her, his smile always ready, made her feel as though she had slipped into a harbor where she was safe.

But the same thing that comforted her also worried her. He offered safety—just as her brothers had always done. Still, life was supposed to be about risk, adventure and exploration.

"It was a lovely evening," she said, deciding that she didn't feel like any of those things tonight. Right now, she wanted the harbor. "Dinner was wonderful."

"Thank you," he said. He continued to scan her features, as though looking for an answer he couldn't find. He came closer to take her chin between his thumb and forefinger. "Did someone upset you?"

She rested her hands lightly at his waist. "Yes, but not deliberately. It was Nattie."

He raised an eyebrow. "Nattie seems to have great affection for you."

"She does. She said she was jealous of the way you look at me."

"And what way is that?"

"Possessively."

He pinched her chin and then released it. "And you're resenting that because you've decided that it's over between us?"

She retained her hold on him. "No," she replied candidly. "I guess I resent that because I know it *isn't* over."

He frowned and looped his arms loosely around her. "I don't understand."

She sighed and leaned in to him. "Neither do I. Shall we just make love and try to understand it later?"

HE DIDN'T HAVE TO THINK about that twice. He lifted her into his arms and carried her off to bed.

Hours later, he lay with her wrapped in his arms, her bottom tucked against him where he still ached for her, and wondered what had possessed her tonight. She'd made love to him like a woman trying to assume control.

Part of the time, he'd fought her for control because he'd taken charge of things his entire life. But the rest of the time he'd enjoyed the test of wills and the occasional surrender to a fate that was deliciously predictable.

And she had seemed to take pleasure in everything—the battles she'd won and the battles he'd wrested from her. He wondered if she understood that there had been no loser tonight.

CHAPTER TWELVE

SAL DIDN'T UNDERSTAND why Dori seemed even more troubled the following morning. She usually glowed after their lovemaking, but today she was all business in a buttoned-to-the-neck robe she'd borrowed from Harper's closet. She fed the baby, poured coffee for her family, and brought him a cup, as he turned pancakes on the griddle, unable to send Charlie off with just a bowl of cereal.

"Thank you," he said, taking it from her.

He didn't think she'd heard him. Because when she wasn't all business, she seemed completely unfocused. He didn't know what to think.

She'd admitted last night that she still loved him, but she hadn't seemed entirely pleased about it.

There were hugs and goodbyes after breakfast. Natalie teased them by carrying the baby out with her and pretending to put him in the car.

"Give me back that baby!" Dori teased in return. They'd hugged each other, and then Natalie had climbed into the van.

"We'll see you next week for my birthday," her mother said. "You are coming to Edenfield, aren't you?"

Dori looked stricken for a moment, then smiled

widely and hugged her mother. "Wouldn't miss it. You drive safely, Dad."

"Always," he said.

Sal stood with his arm around Dori and Max, as they waved her family off.

"Mom's birthday!" Dori said urgently the moment the van was out of sight. "I was supposed to plan a party and I forgot! What'll I do?"

"You mean a party at a restaurant?"

"I don't know. It was supposed to be up to me."

Now she looked distressed. He followed her back into the house. "I was supposed to write my book, assert myself as an independent member of the McKeon family, and I end up with a baby, a husband and terminal confusion!" She glowered at him as though it were all his fault. "And no party!"

"We can pull it together in a week," Sal said bracingly. He could see that she wanted to believe him.

"You think?" she asked.

He was about to reassure her that he did, when the phone rang. She picked up the cordless from the coffee table. Max was pulling at Dori's hair, so Sal took the baby from her, put him in the playpen in the kitchen and handed him one of the soft toys he loved to examine.

Sal was clearing away the table when Dori appeared in the kitchen doorway, her distress hiked up a notch.

"What?" he asked, preparing himself.

"Duncan's been asked to replace Harrison Ford in the fourth *Raiders* movie," she said tightly. "So the family had to come back from Europe early."

"All of them?"

"Every last one. They called from Chicago. They'll be here tonight, and they asked me to see if I can get the folks here for the next few days, because Duncan has to leave for Africa on Sunday. So we're moving up the birthday party."

"Can you reach your parents?"

She held up the cordless phone. "I called them on their cell phone. They'll come right back after they drop my aunt and my cousin off at the airport."

"Uh-oh."

"We're not going to get it pulled together in eight hours, are we? And I still don't have a present!"

She ran from the room, sobbing.

He stared for a moment at the spot where she'd been. Then he moved Max and the playpen out into the living room and within sight of Cheddar, who slept on the back of the sofa and could always entertain Max, even in his sleep. Sal went toward the bedroom and the sound of sniffling and hiccuping.

He peered around the half-open door and saw Dori standing in simple white bra and panties, slapping through the things in the closet.

"You want to talk about it?" he asked, leaning against the doorway.

She yanked out a sweater and pair of jeans. She sniffed and drew a breath probably intended to help her get control. "No, thank you," she replied with stiff courtesy. "Talking only makes it worse."

"Makes what worse?"

"The confusion." She pulled the sweater over her head. Her short hair stood up in spikes.

"Which confusion?"

She gave him a quelling look as she fell onto the edge of the bed and pulled on her jeans. "Sal, this is talking."

"True. It's just hard for me to stand by, while you're clearly upset, and do nothing."

The jeans pulled up as far as she could manage sitting down, she stood, fitted them up to her waist and zipped the fly. "Well, there's nothing you can do about this," she said, sitting down again to pull on a pair of ankle socks. "I'm just disappointed in myself. And much as you'd like to protect me from everything, there's nothing you can do about that."

"You know," he said, trying to sound reasonable when he really wanted to shake her, "I can't see where you have any reason to be disappointed. You might not have gotten as much work done on your book as you'd planned, but you had a baby in the house, one you've kept and cared for by choice."

"Actually, you did most of that," she corrected. "And I'm not disappointed about the book or the baby, or anything." She pulled on a tennis shoe, stomped her foot to the floor and leaned over to tie it.

"Then what's left?" he asked.

She pushed herself up and hobbled toward him, one shoe on, one shoe off, a storm raging in her eyes. "*You're* what's left!" she said. "I was going to have my life under control by September, but I'll never accomplish that if I don't have my feelings for you under control!"

Ah. He liked the sound of that. He knew it was

important to remain cool. "But feelings can't be controlled, as a rule. We can control the way we react to them, but we can't control *them.*"

She spread her arms and let them fall to her side. "Oh, don't get technical! I don't care! I just want to feel that at twenty-six years old I know what I'm doing with my life."

"What do you want to do with it?"

She went back to the bed and sat down to put her other sock and shoe on. "I want Max, but I don't want to stomp all over Brenda Ward's rights if she simply screwed up one time."

"Well...that's noble."

She was silent while she put on and tied her second shoe. Then she stood up, folded her arms and looked at him defensively from the middle of the bedroom. "And I want to live with you, but I don't want you to feel possessive about me."

He could say something conciliatory, but their life together was at stake. "Well. There we have a problem," he said.

She turned to the mirror over the dresser and ran her fingers through her hair. Some of the spikes lay down and others sprang up. "I know. And I want personal freedom to do as I please without recriminations from anyone. I want that more than I want anything."

"Then I guess we're at an impasse."

She looked away from the mirror and snatched her purse up off the bed. "I guess we are."

She looked weary, but not entirely defeated. He took that as a good sign.

"I have to go shopping for a birthday present, get some party stuff, lay in some groceries. I suppose you're going to insist on coming."

He smiled. "You're not suffering confusion on that score. Let me make sure everything's turned off in the kitchen."

DORI GRABBED the diaper bag, the money safely stashed in a shoe pouch in the bottom of the closet, pulled Max out of the playpen, and carried him out to the car. Sal followed.

She put Max into his car seat, while Sal stashed the stroller frame in the trunk.

"If you're in a temper, maybe I should drive," Sal suggested, grinning at her over the top of the car. "Anger and your lead foot are not a good combination."

He was teasing, she knew, but she wasn't prepared to be charmed out of her depression. "Fine," she said. "I want to go to the antique shop. Maybe they'll have some really ugly new stock."

"We can only hope."

"Miss McKeon!" the clerk said, familiar with her now that she'd been back several times in search of the right gift for her parents. "We have a new shipment from a dealer in England. There might be something you'll like."

He walked her around the large room, while Sal stayed nearby with Max.

The clerk showed her beautiful jewelry that was not only too beautiful to appeal to her parents, but too costly for her budget. There was a piece of art deco glass that was interesting but a little austere for her the-more-ruffles-and-doo-dads-the-better parents. She studied a regimental helmet that was beautiful, but too significant, and an ugly dish stand worth considering if she couldn't find anything else.

And then she saw it.

"It's a Mayan jaguar head from Mexico," the clerk said, embellishing as he noted her excitement. "About 600 AD."

"Stone?" Dori asked, running her fingertips along the small figure's large ears and the sharp teeth visible in the open mouth. He was ugly, but somehow appealing.

"Yes," the clerk replied. "It was found outside Mexico City, I understand."

"Sal!" Dori called, taking the stone head carefully into her hands. "Look at this. It's a jaguar from Mexico."

He nodded over the find. "He's ugly, all right," he agreed. "But have your parents ever collected anything that wasn't American or European?"

Dori ran through a mental list of everything in her parents' home, things that had been given to her and her brothers, and things they'd brought to the beach house.

"I don't think so," she replied, "but it wouldn't be bad to start them on something new, would it?"

"Not at all."

Dori handed it to the clerk, elated. "I'll take it."

The clerk wrapped the head in bubble wrap, then tissue, placed it carefully in a box and gift-wrapped it.

The treasure clutched in her arms, Dori led the way out the front door. I'll buy you an espresso," she said to Sal. "Then I have to get some paper plates and napkins, order a cake and buy lots of groceries. We have a lot of people to feed."

"I'm at your service," Sal assured her. "See? You're not the only one enslaved."

She gave him a stern look. "No smart remarks, okay?"

"Sorry." He followed her into the coffee bar at the Buckley Arms and settled her at a small round table. "You seemed a little more cheerful. I thought you were feeling less confused."

She sat with the baby in her lap and pushed everything within reach to the other side of the table. "I think this is just a shopper's high. I'm still confused about us."

"I see. You want a mocha?"

"Please? And one of those little chocolate mice things you bought me the last time."

"Are you going to bite the head off again?"

She nodded. "And I'll probably mutilate the licorice tail, too, so you might want to sit at another table."

"Remember that the baby's impressionable."

With a grudging smile, she put her fingertip to the baby's nose. He caught her hand in his two and pulled her finger into his little mouth.

As Sal went to the counter, she rocked the baby gently, trying to ignore the little saw-teeth working into her knuckle. She couldn't believe how much she'd come to love Max in such a short time. She had what Sal had termed the "noble intention" of making certain Brenda had a fair chance when she was found, but Dori truly didn't know what she'd do if Brenda wanted the baby back.

And then there was Sal. She watched him waiting at the counter, his eyes scanning the street beyond the window, ever the bodyguard.

She loved him desperately. Now that she understood why he'd left her on their wedding day, she could understand and accept his actions. She could even accept the blame for their two years apart.

She also knew that he loved her; he'd been the perfect father to Max, and the perfect husband since they'd come back from Seattle together. Except for that possessive quality that made him second-guess her decisions, and even reverse them if he felt he should.

After finally ridding herself somewhat of the yoke of her brothers' protection, she didn't think she could live with that again.

Sal returned to the table with her drink and his, a white paper bag trapped between his fingers and her cup. A curious prickling took place throughout her body as he placed her cup at the farthest reach of her hand and out of the baby's way. He never forgot to think about Max.

He put his own cup down right near hers, handed her the bag, then took Max from her as his grasping little hands reached for the paper.

She pulled out a sugar cookie.

"That's ours," Sal said, reaching across the table for it.

Her chocolate mouse was on the bottom. She ate it slowly, with relish, deliberately biting the head off when Sal glanced her way. He laughed and shared tiny bites of the cookie with the baby. Max's feet kicked and his hands pounded the table in his excitement over the treat.

They stocked up on an enormous amount of food, for which Dori knew her brothers would reimburse her when they arrived. She ordered a cake in the market's bakery, bought paper goods and found a card to go with her gift.

Shopping took several hours, and finally Max, who'd grown tired and fussy, was fast asleep on Dori's shoulder. Sal pushed a large cart filled with their purchases across the street to the parking lot behind the antique shop.

"I hope there's enough room in the car for all this," Dori said. "And, please, no cracks about strapping me to the roof."

He grinned as he pushed the cart. "You'd make a very seductive hood ornament."

"Sweet of you. If there isn't enough room, I'm leaving you with the baby, hauling everything home, then coming back for you. And I don't care about your bodyguard rule about never leaving your cli—"

At that very moment, a dark van pulled up right in front of them with a screech of tires.

Sal turned her and the baby in the other direction. "Run!" he ordered, as four young men and a young woman leapt out of the van. Brenda and her friends.

Dori didn't remember ever feeling so torn in her

entire life. She wanted to protect the baby, but she didn't want to leave Sal.

"Go!" Sal shouted at her again, pushing her, trying to cover her retreat.

She made the decision to stay. She wrapped her arms around Max and stood her ground, in the belief that Brenda would never hurt her own baby.

WHEN THIS WAS OVER, Sal thought, he and Dori were having a firm talk about the principle of cooperation in a crisis.

He should have been more watchful, he berated himself as he got squarely in front of Dori and Max. But he'd been worried about Dori's mood, worried about what she was thinking, worried that she'd decide it really was over between them, and that he'd have no recourse but to tie her up and take her home with him and Max as freight on a flight to Seattle.

The four young men fanned out, street punks with baseball hats on backward and sleeves rolled up to show off tattoos of a shark's head.

The young woman ran around them to take the baby from Dori. She was pale, with yards of dark hair and an expression of hopelessness. She wore pencil-slim jeans and a short-cropped leather jacket.

"Brenda!" Dori whispered as she clutched at Max. "Get Max out of the way!"

"Dori." Brenda hesitated as though she would have said something, but Dori pushed her to the side.

"Get out of the way!" the tallest of the young men barked at her. Valdefiero—he'd been the face at the window, Sal guessed.

Brenda backed away, stopping several yards away from them, the baby clutched to her.

Sal had the Smith & Wesson in his waistband, but there had to be a better way out of this. "What do you want?" he asked.

Dori had moved to stand beside him but he pushed her back behind him.

"You know what I want." The kid came to stand right in front of him. Dark hair stuck through the sizing hole in his hat, and he had a silver stud in his nose. He had a baby-fine mustache and sloping shoulders under a Grateful Dead T-shirt.

The punk was measuring him, Sal decided, as shoe-button black eyes roved over him from head to toe. He was trying to decide if the eighteen or twenty years Sal had on him would make the older man tired and weaker, or stronger and more experienced. He didn't seem to be able to decide.

"What you *should* want," Sal said, indicating Brenda, "your girlfriend has already taken."

Valdefiero shook his head. "I want the money."

"I understand the church got the money back."

"Yeah, so the way I figure it, you'd better come up with $11,572 for *me*."

Dori peered around Sal. "You stole from a church!" she accused.

The punk blinked. "Of course I stole from a church. No security guards. Now, give me my money."

"What do you intend to do with it?"

The kid rolled his eyes. "Mend my ways and start over," he said in tones of bored sarcasm. "Maybe go to college. Establish a fund for underprivileged children. What do you *think* I intend to do with it?" His voice rose and his indolence took on a dangerous edge. "My friends and I are going to drink and bed girls until it's gone."

Brenda took a step toward him. Dori moved around Sal, presumably to reach for the baby, but Sal caught her arm.

"You told me we were going to California," Brenda said.

"And you told me," Dori said to Brenda, "that you were going to turn the money in to the police."

Valdefiero shook his head pityingly. "That's what I told her to tell you." Then he turned on Brenda. "You stole my money!" he roared at her. "Did you really think I'd take you anywhere? We only brought you along because you know this chick's car."

"You were wrong to take the money," Brenda said, tears in her voice, "and I took it from you to make a better life for our son."

"How many times do I have to tell you? I don't want a son. I don't want a woman. At least, not a woman who hangs on."

"Brenda," Dori called, reaching an arm out to the girl. "Come here and stand with us."

Brenda looked from the man she'd trusted to Dori and Sal.

"Come on," Dori encouraged. "Someday you'll be proud you took the stand."

Brenda, looking uncertain, came to stand beside them. Dori put an arm around her. Max, now awake, leaned out of Brenda's arms and cried for Dori, but Brenda held on to him.

"What is this?" Valdefiero demanded. "Some stupid line in the sand crap? You got two women, a baby and an old guy against the four of us. What do you think you're going to do with that?"

Apparently impatient with the turn of events, he swung at Sal. But it was the "old guy" crack and not the swing that did it. Sal knocked him out cold.

The other three punks looked at each other. Before they could decide what to do, a Jeep pulled up behind them, and they scattered.

Sal tackled one, and Bram, leaping out of the Jeep, chased the other one down. The third one got away.

Bram tossed Dori a cell phone as he struggled to cuff his quarry. She dialed 911 and told the dispatcher that they had three of the four men who'd stolen the money from Faith Community Church.

WHEN DORI LOOKED UP, Brenda was gone.

She felt her heart snap in two. Oh, God. She'd known she was taking a chance, but she'd wanted to believe that Brenda had the baby's best interests at heart—and that Brenda knew giving him to Dori was in Max's best interest.

She started to cry, large gulping sobs that came from deep inside and felt as though they churned up everything in her chest.

Sal came and caught her arm, drawing her with him toward the red car. "Come on. We'll find her," he said.

She wanted to do just that, but she really understood for the first time what it was like for a mother to have her child ripped from her arms—either physically, or by circumstances she was powerless to prevent. Still, the baby wasn't safe with a biological mother who couldn't make sound decisions.

The police arrived, and Will Valdefiero was put into the back of one police car, his two companions into another.

Bram came to them. "We have to go to the station," he said, frowning in concern at Dori. "Did she get hurt?" he asked Sal.

"Brenda took off with the baby," Sal explained. "Take Dori, I'm going after—"

Bram shook his head. "The police are putting out an APB for her right now. They'll find her. I followed them here and was just waiting for someone to make a move."

Dori pulled herself together, discovering that "together" wasn't quite the same as it had been just half an hour ago. Now there was a hole where her heart had been.

She leaned in to Sal, and they started for the car.

"Oh, wait." Sal pointed to the cart. "The groceries. Bram, can we drop those off at Dori's first? The whole family's coming home tonight, and we've got a couple of hundred dollars' worth of food here."

"Uh, sure. Just get there as soon as you can." He leaned closer to say quietly, "And you'd better bring the cash. I know you replaced it, but the police will..."

"Sure," Sal said. "See you at the station."

They had stashed groceries everywhere—the trunk,

the floor and the back seat. Dori burst into tears anew at the sight of the empty car seat.

She sounded as though she were going to die, and Sal thought the sound of her grief would kill him, too. His own distress over Max was eating away at him.

When they arrived at the beach house, Dori's parents, home from the airport, came out to help with the groceries. Sal explained briefly what had happened, while Dori fell apart in her mother's arms. Peg wept with her. Sal and Charlie, jaws set, made a dozen trips from the car to the kitchen and back again.

All the groceries finally stowed, Dori washed her face and, composed again, went with Sal to the police station. They told their stories in a small, pale-green office, where they were given paper cups of strong coffee. When they were finally finished with their reports, an attractive young woman in a dark blue suit stepped inside the office.

"Mr. and Mrs. Dominguez?" she asked.

Dori's eyes were glazed, but Sal responded, "Yes."

She smiled. "I'm from Adult and Family Services," she said. "May I speak to you when you're finished here?"

"They're finished," the officer said. "Here. You can have the office. I have a few calls to make."

"Good. Well." The young woman put her purse on the desk, then smiled at each of them in turn. "I'll be right back. I know you've had a long afternoon, but I'll be very quick."

Dori put a hand to her forehead. "I have Riverdance going on in my head," she said to Sal with a wince.

"You have Tylenol in your purse," he reminded her, going to a water cooler in a corner of the office. "You gave me one the other day."

She located the bottle in her purse, then fumbled, seemingly unable to open it. He handed her the cup of water, took the bottle from her and handed her two pills. She popped them in her mouth and drank. "I suppose she needs information on Brenda," she said.

"I suppose," he replied.

Sal had the selfish thought that, because Dori seemed so distraught, she might decide that she needed him, after all, whether or not he was possessive.

Then he knew with certainty that if it was a choice between that or getting Max back for her, he'd find the baby.

With that in mind, he thought he was hallucinating when the office door opened again and the AFS woman walked in with Max in her arms.

Dori, even with her back to the door, sensed Max's presence immediately and ran to him with a cry of delight. "Max!" she squealed, taking him from the woman. "What happened? Where's his mother?"

"Brenda Ward has been an emancipated minor for the past year," the woman said. "Her mother died, her father's alcoholic, and she was better off on her own, or so we'd hoped. The boyfriend wasn't a good choice, but she came to me about an hour ago with Max, here, and gave me instructions to take him to you and Mr. Dominguez. We'll be filing release papers tomorrow, and she wants you to adopt him."

"She's...sure?" Dori wept, hugging Max, who squealed in protest.

"Positive. She recognizes that though she loved him, she was a poor mother. We'll have to see what the judge says about her letting Valdefiero into the parsonage, but she wants to get her GED, go to college, and be smart—like you are." The woman delivered that last with a smile. "She admires you. She says you were kind to her."

"I gave her a candy bar," Dori said, taking the handkerchief Sal handed her. "Such a small thing."

"To a person who has nothing," the woman insisted, "that's a big thing. So I've arranged for Max to stay with you until you can get his adoption under way."

Dori nodded. "I'll see an attorney tomorrow."

The woman turned to Sal. "I guess we're just presuming you're in agreement with all this."

"I am," he said, striking a tone intended to convince her that he figured in the decision.

"Good." She handed him her card. "If there's anything I can do, please let me know. And keep me apprised of the adoption proceedings."

"We will," Dori promised.

Max reached for Sal. He took him and, with an arm around Dori, walked out to the car. During the entire ride home, Dori peered around her seat and stared at Max.

At home there were Airport Rental cars everywhere and a virtual tide of humanity ran out of the house to greet them. Her parents and her brothers, looking worried, came first. At the sight of the baby in the back seat, there was an urgent discussion.

Dori opened her door before Sal turned off the motor, and her mother demanded, "The mother brought him back? Do you get to keep him?"

"I do!" Dori shouted. "She gave him up to me. She's signing release papers tomorrow, and I'm getting a lawyer to file for adoption."

There were shouts and screams of excitement and congratulations, hugs and tears.

Sal wanted to skulk away and find a way to stay sane until he knew for certain whether the adoption was all she was going to have the lawyer file for tomorrow. He couldn't possibly ask her tonight, with her whole family here to celebrate her mother's birthday.

But Skye and Harper, Dori's sisters-in-law, were upon him, offering their congratulations. Peg had apparently explained about the baby and about his spending the last week-and-a-half with Dori. And she'd passed on what she thought to be true—that Sal and Dori had rediscovered their love. Everyone seemed happy about that so he could find no escape.

Tall, brunette Skye, and small, blond Harper each caught one of his arms and led him around the car to their husbands. Darrick and Dillon had the dark, handsome stamp of the McKeons.

Darrick shook his hand and frowned. "You married our sister without inviting us to the wedding?"

Before Sal could explain, Dillon also shook his hand. "Thanks, buddy. I'm getting to hate weddings.

And Mom assures us that Dori looks happy, so you must be treating her well."

"Doing my best," he assured him carefully.

"Sal!" Julie, his cousin, small and dark-haired, flew out of the crowd and into his arms. They'd been carefree children together, then budding criminals, then young people forced to make a choice between their families and their futures. She'd bravely chosen her future, and he'd done his best to see that she didn't lose her family.

"I can't believe this!" she squealed in his ear. "You're married to my best friend! And you're my brother-in-law!"

The family was all crowded around, the children in a second layer like the exotic undergrowth in a forest. Max was being passed around. Sal caught Dori's pleading eyes in the middle of the group.

"Yes, I am," he agreed. "And I've had a very trying afternoon. If anyone has a lead on a Bloody Mary, I'd be very grateful."

"Come with me." Duncan, Julie's husband, put an arm around Sal's shoulders, led him into the living room and pushed him into an overstuffed chair. "I understand you've been cooking since you've been here. Well, you just relax, because Dillon and the ladies are now in charge." He pinched Dori's cheek as she passed him. "The ladies who can cook, that is. Sit right here—someone will bring you a drink. And dinner will be ready in under an hour."

"*Madre de Dios,*" he said. "I'm home."

DORI WAS QUIVERING. She remembered that the same thing had happened to her the night she'd seen Valdefiero's face at the window.

They'd had dinner, and then they all sat around in the living room, adults on sofas and chairs and on the floor, children on the backs and arms of sofas and chairs and in the laps of aunts and uncles. They'd talked about the trip to Europe, about Dori's book, about the hospital in Madre Maria, about the big birthday bash tomorrow. Cheddar, delighted with the new variety of laps, large and small, tried them all.

Dori had been keeping a low profile, not wanting anyone to know that she was jelly inside. Fortunately, she was holding Duncan and Julie's three-year-old twins, who were sprawled all over her in a sleepy stupor and didn't seem to notice.

She was going to have to admit that she hadn't planned anything. But before she could, Julie, sitting on the arm of Duncan's chair, said, "Why don't we just have it here? I mean, Dori wouldn't have had time to plan anything with the baby and the worry about the thief, and we can't make reservations for so many of us at the last minute. Can't we just have it in the backyard and be gluttonous and noisy?"

"That sounds wonderful to me," Peg said. "Doesn't it, Charlie?"

"Of course it does." Charlie sat with his leg propped on an ottoman, Harper and Dillon's Darian and Danielle asleep in his lap. "But it's your birthday, Peg."

"We missed beer and brots for the Fourth of July," Dillon said. "And Mom likes that as much as we do. Why don't we do that?"

Dori congratulated herself for having bought ten pounds of brot.

Peg led the unanimous cheer of approval.

"A few salads," Harper added, "a few desserts. It'll be a feast!"

More cheers of approval. Then the adults began to gather up children and wander off to bed. Darrick had to peel David, ten, and Drake, five, from Sal, who sat on the floor with one boy asleep against each shoulder.

"Since you've got the baby and you need access to the fridge," Julie said to Dori, trading her a sleeping Max for one of the twins, "Duncan and the girls and I will sleep in your attic room, the folks can have our room, and you two can still have the downstairs bedroom."

Duncan came to get Gabrielle. Everyone involved in the game of musical rooms nodded approval.

Dori took a hot shower, while Sal put Max down in the crib. She'd hoped the heat would calm her, but nothing seemed to help. She needed…something.

Sal was waiting outside the shower in his nighttime attire of jogging shorts and T-shirt, with a towel and a brandy.

When she looked surprised, he handed her the brandy and wrapped the towel around her, rubbing her dry through the thick folds. "I was afraid you were going to fly apart while we were discussing the party," he said. "Fortunately, everyone was too excited and too happy to be together to notice."

"I don't know…what's the matter with me," she

said, her teeth now chattering. "Max is fine. I'm... I'm fine."

"Just post-crisis reaction," he said. "Drink that, come to bed, and you'll be fine."

"You're sure?"

"I'm sure."

She drank and coughed, drank and choked, and drank and finally enjoyed it.

"That's the trouble with brandy," she said, handing back the glass and pulling on her cotton nightshirt. "By the time it's sedated you enough for you to enjoy it, it's gone."

"Very philosophical," he said. "I suppose life's a little like that."

She climbed into bed as he turned off the light. He gathered her into his arms, pulled her back against his chest and burrowed his nose in her hair. Somewhere above her on the pillow, Cheddar purred like a little engine.

"Everything's all right, *querida*," he said softly. "You have what you want now. Be easy. Everything's all right."

It was. She knew it was. Everything was all right.

But something was missing.

She wanted to understand about...about a man owning a woman. How ownership could possibly relate to love. But she couldn't focus, couldn't remember...

She held on to the arms wrapped around her and fell asleep.

CHAPTER THIRTEEN

DORI'S FIRST THOUGHT upon awakening the following morning was, did she *have* to understand it? Sal loved her, and she loved him. She enjoyed his company so much because there was friendship as well as passion in their feelings for each other.

She just wondered if she could adjust to that possessive quality in him, or if he'd be able to cope with her resistance to it. Many marriages based on love in the beginning eventually fell apart because of some difference that hadn't been addressed. And the last thing she wanted to do was fail at marriage, when everyone else in her family was so good at it.

Sal was already up when she climbed out of bed, and Dori discovered that Max's crib was empty. Cheddar had also left her. The buzz of conversation came from beyond her closed bedroom door. Apparently most of the family were up and having breakfast.

The first thing Dori did was call Athena Hartford's office and schedule an appointment for the following afternoon to talk about Max's adoption.

"Adoption?" Athena asked in surprise. "I thought we were going to talk about divorce."

Dori groaned. "It's complicated," she said. "I'll see you at two-thirty tomorrow."

"Okay," Athena agreed. "I'll be ready."

Dori showered quickly and dressed in jeans and a light blue camp shirt. She made the bed and tidied the bedroom, realizing grimly that she was reluctant to go out and be with her family.

She squared her shoulders and looked at herself in the mirror. "You had been getting it together," she told herself firmly. "It isn't your fault that a baby and husband slowed you down. Well, the husband might have been your fault, but his reappearance wasn't. Well, not entirely. You did go and seek him out, but that was because of the baby. Okay, let it go. You're starting to confuse yourself further. And confusion's the whole issue right now, isn't it?"

It was hard not to be confused around her family. They were charming but forceful people. Just like Sal.

A quick rap on the door was followed by Sal's entrance. "Eggs?" he asked, "or French toast—since you didn't really get to eat yours yesterday? Harper's asking."

Dori felt contrary. Not quarrelsome precisely, because she didn't want to fight with anyone, but she didn't feel like doing things the way they were usually done. If she was feeling confusion, she may as well go with it.

"Is there ice cream?" she asked.

He arched an eyebrow. "Uh, I think so. Coffee-fudge something."

She smiled as she came toward him. "Coffee

sounds like a good breakfast flavor. I'll have two scoops, please."

"Of ice cream."

"Yes."

"For breakfast."

"Yes." She stopped in the doorway, a hand on her hip. "You're not going to try to countermand that, are you?"

"No. I wouldn't think of it." He held the door open and stood back to let her through.

The house was in a kind of cheerful chaos. Most of the children were sitting at the kitchen table, except for David, who was watching baseball in the living room with his grandfather.

The cousins were having a riotous time. Max was kicking and squealing and trying to feed himself crumbled pieces of scrambled egg. Skye and Julie were attempting to maintain some sort of order.

The three-year-old twins in matching pink shorts sets, with tea towels tied around their necks, sat in kitchen chairs, their little heads barely visible above the table. It didn't stop their enthusiastic devouring of toast and jam and milk in cups with training lids.

Danielle sat in Skye's lap messily eating a banana, and it was Skye who wore the tea towel. Drake and Darian ate Cheerios in milk, Darian holding two of the little disks up to his eyes and delighting his cousins.

Harper, manning a frying pan, greeted Dori with a cheerful "Good morning. What'll it be?"

"Ice cream," Dori replied, going to the freezer for the carton.

Darian looked at his mother as though his faith in adults had just collapsed. "How come Aunt Dori gets to have ice cream for breakfast," he demanded, "and we gots cereal?"

"Yeah!" Drake supported his protest.

Harper sent Dori a reprimanding glance. "Thanks, Aunt Dori," she said, then added to the children, "Aunt Dori is a grown-up and doesn't have to worry about building strong bones and teeth. When you're an adult, you can have ice cream for breakfast if you want to. But Uncle Sal's going to have a healthy breakfast, aren't you, Uncle Sal."

"Yes, I am," Sal replied stoutly. "Eggs and toast and orange juice."

"*We* couldn't have any juice!" Drake reported in an affronted tone.

"Ixnay on the uicejay," Julie said, holding up the empty carton. She added in a whisper, "One too many screwdrivers last night."

"Ah. Just coffee, then," Sal conceded.

"Good man." Julie pulled a cup down and poured it for him, while Dori pulled an ice cream scoop out of the drawer.

"There's apple juice concentrate in the freezer," Dori said to the boys, momentarily abandoning her ice cream. "Want me to make you some?"

The boys chorused an affirmative.

She mixed it up quickly, stirred vigorously, then poured juice into glasses for Darian, Drake and the twins, and into the bottles for Danielle and Max.

She poured the last few ounces in the pitcher into

a glass for Sal. "There you go. You'll have to pretend it's orange."

"I can do that," he said quietly. "We've been pretending a lot of things since I've been here."

She didn't want to get into that. She put the pitcher in the bottom of the dishwasher, scooped up her ice cream and wandered out into the backyard.

Her brothers had carried chairs outside, and Darrick was scrubbing the picnic table, while Dillon and Duncan hauled the second one out of the garage.

"If you got another scrubber," Darrick said to her, indicating the second table, "you could clean off that one and help me put up the umbrellas."

"I could." She ate a spoonful of ice cream and went to sit in the middle of the hammock, legs folded pretzel-style.

He stopped in his work to lean both hands on the table and look at her. "But, you're not going to?"

She turned to him, dipping her spoon into her cup again. "That's why you're such a good administrator. You're so quick."

"I'm a good administrator," he said ominously, "because I don't take guff from anyone."

"Except Skye," Dillon replied, as he and Duncan crabwalked with the table past the hammock.

"He has to be nice to her," Duncan explained, grunting as they set the table down. "She once crashed him in an airplane and keeps threatening to do it again. Dori, go get us something to clean this off with."

"You go get it," she said, scraping the last little bit of ice cream out of the bottom of the cup.

"You've been on vacation for a month, while I've been writing a brilliant book."

"What," Duncan asked in surprise, turning to his brother, "has happened to our sweet little sister?"

Dillon frowned at him. "What family do you belong to? We've never had a sweet little sister."

"Well, she used to be willing to help us."

"When was that?"

"Not since she was little," Darrick put in. "Since she turned twelve, she's been nothing but mouth and attitude."

Dori lay back in the hammock with a contented sigh, letting her hand with the cup fall over the side until she could drop the cup to the grass.

"I had three very bad examples," she said, getting comfortable. "So there's no way you can blame me."

"We know Sal didn't make her this way," she heard Duncan speculate. "He's the epitome of suave good manners."

"Well, she is half Mom, you know," Dillon said.

"We all are," Duncan argued, "and we're not spoiled rotten like she is."

"Ha!" Dori exclaimed without opening her eyes. "You have to see the three of you from my perspective—always calling the shots, always getting in my way, always terrifying my boyfriends."

"I think we did pretty well on that score," Duncan said. "We did approve Sal, and he's the one you finally chose—even if you didn't tell us about it for two whole years."

She opened her eyes and sighed. "Well, we got

married and then he was gone. For two whole years it was like we weren't married."

"But your marriage is working now." It wasn't a question. Dillon said it as though he wanted reassurance that it was true.

She sat up again and folded her legs. The hammock swung gently. "Mostly," she replied.

Darrick came closer. "I don't like the sound of that. What do you mean, mostly?"

The three of them were now lined up beside her in various poses of fraternal displeasure—Dillon leaning on the base at the foot of the hammock; Duncan, arms folded, frowning near her feet; Darrick right beside her, hands in his pockets.

"This is precisely it!" she said with sudden vehemence, angry that they'd messed up her contrary but mellow morning. "He's just like the three of you. And he does exactly this same thing when he doesn't agree with something I've done. He's always convinced that *I'm* wrong, and that he can explain to me how it should be, or fix it for me, whichever course will bring about the least argument."

Darrick frowned at her as though trying to figure out how that was bad. "So, yours is the only opinion allowed," he asked, "and presumed to be right?"

"No. But I'm *allowed* to be wrong without someone having to fix it."

Dillon, the doctor and a scientist at heart, didn't understand that at all. "Why would you want to remain wrong, if someone could help you make it right?"

She closed her eyes in exasperation. "Because I

have the personal freedom to *be* wrong. It's my right! And my point is that I'm not *always* wrong! But if you don't agree with me, you presume I am.''

Duncan narrowed his eyes. ''I don't think that's true. The only time we interfere is if we think you're in danger. And that whole mess surrounding the Julie incident should have proven to you that you should have come to us for help in the first place.''

She growled, too exasperated to form words. ''I didn't come to you,'' she said slowly, as though to simple children, ''because Julie didn't want you to interfere—and I knew that was exactly what you'd do. I can't believe that even now, three years later, you still don't see that!''

''What I see,'' Darrick said, ''is that you seem to think brothers and husbands should sit around like potted plants and stay out of your life because you don't want interference. If you help us because you're a woman, it's okay. But if we help you because we're men, we're taking over.''

''Help and interference are not the same thing,'' she pointed out.

''So, we've interfered with you more than we've helped?'' Duncan asked.

She was beginning to regret the entire conversation. ''Can we just drop it?'' she asked. She lay back again and closed her eyes. ''I came out here just to mellow out a little and think things through.''

''Really.'' She heard Duncan sigh, his voice moving slightly away from her as he said to Darrick and Dillon, ''No small surprise her marriage is only *mostly* working.''

She ignored the jibe and her confused, hurt feelings and kept her eyes closed, hoping her brothers were moving toward the house and would leave her to her thoughts—

A moment later, the hammock made a wide swinging motion. She opened her eyes and tried to sit up, but she was rocked backward as the woven rope suddenly surrounded her.

DORI WAS GOING to torture and then kill every one of her brothers before they went home tomorrow. She'd been hanging in the ash tree for the past five minutes like some trapped jungle creature in *Hatari!*, a good six or seven feet off the ground. During that time she'd been carefully making plans. Fraternal retribution was one thing, but they'd gone too far this time.

She refused to call for help for fear someone would come and see her humiliation. So she sat silently, trapped in her net prison, brooding, one foot caught in the mesh.

"Oh, no." She heard the screen door slam and dropped her head on her arms, which were folded over one bent knee.

"You're lucky I don't call Harper to immortalize you in a photograph," Julie said, looking up at her.

"If you're going to gloat," Dori said, "go away."

"I'm not gloating." Julie sounded offended. "Duncan sent me out here to talk to you. He said you wouldn't resent it because I'm another woman."

Dori did feel resentful but couldn't determine whether it was because she'd have resented anyone trying to change her mind about anything, or because she was hanging in a tree.

"So, what's the problem?" Julie asked. "Why have they hung you in a tree like an old float from a fishing net?"

Dori relayed most of their conversation. "Does Duncan interfere with what you want to do all the time?" she asked. "And if he does, how do you stand it?"

"Hmm." Julie sat down on the grass as though she were simply having a conversation with someone sitting across from her at a kitchen table. "Subordinating your will is always an adjustment. And I never do it on big things. I fight for what I believe in, but I also believe Duncan has the right to argue for his point—even if it differs from mine. But if we're dealing with nothing really significant, I sometimes do what he wants just because I know he'll be more peaceful about it, and I love him, and peace is what I want for him."

Julie laughed lightly. "But being the scrapper that you are, you probably don't get that, do you."

"I don't know," Dori admitted. "I'd like to, but why shouldn't *he* give in? Why don't you get to be the one at peace?"

"Because when you love each other, one of you is always conceding to the other. It's what makes a marriage work. When you intertwine two lives, someone has to give, otherwise the connection is broken. Or you can live parallel lives like some people do and get along just fine, but then I don't think you ever really get to grasp the depths of real love. Giving is the only sure test of it, and when your lives intersect only occasionally, you never know what that other person is willing to do for you on a day-to-day basis—or you for him. Giving builds on itself time after time. But I think if you just walk along side by side, one day you're going to go off in different directions.''

Dori found some sense in that. "I resent Sal's strength because I'd finally broken free of my brothers." She shook her net cage and made a scornful sound. "Or thought I had."

Julie shrugged. "I think love and personal freedom are mutually exclusive. If you want to answer to no one, my advice is don't get married and have children. But I'm a little late with that, I think."

"Julie?"

"Yeah?"

"Can you get me down from here?"

Julie got to her feet and dusted off her hands. "I'll have to get help. Hold on."

"Oh, good advice. I'll just *hang* here until you get back!"

Okay, that all made sense to Dori. Love made its demands. But from what Sal had taught her of love, it was usually well worth it. And maybe she could concede her opinion on minor points if it helped their relationship and his peace of mind.

But...

The back door slammed again, and Sal came sprinting out to stop stock-still in the middle of the yard, staring.

"DORI?" he asked, not quite able to believe his eyes. His wife hung in the ash tree like a queen bee in a hive. "What happened?"

He grabbed a chair and placed it under her.

"A little sibling humor," she said, sounding less annoyed than he'd expected her to be. "Can you get me down?"

He stepped onto the chair, balancing himself by looping his fingers in the netting. He pushed her protruding foot back inside the netting and was about to free her by reaching for the long ends of the hammock looped over a thick branch—when he realized his advantage here.

"Depends," he replied, figuring he had nothing to lose by interrogating her while he had the upper hand, so to speak.

"On what?" she asked in disbelief.

"On whether you made plans to file for divorce as well as adoption when you talked to Athena Hartford this morning."

She sighed. "I'm not filing for divorce."

He felt relief, but only a little. She didn't sound happy about not filing. "Why didn't you?"

"Because I'm not sure it's the right thing."

That wasn't the answer. He'd been a patient man, considering, but that was about to change.

"Then, if you're not sure divorce is the right thing," he concluded, "you're also not sure staying together is the right thing."

"I'm confused!" she shrieked at him. "Aren't you ever confused?"

"Not about you," he said, reaching up to hold on

to the branch above her head as he worked the loop on the front part of the net trap toward the end of the branch.

"Reach your arm out the side," he ordered, "and put it around my neck. Hook your other arm in the netting behind you."

She did as he asked, her floral scent wafting around him, trying to dim his billowing temper. But he was beyond being seduced by a fragrance.

"All right, hold on." He freed the loop, and the front part of the hammock fell between them in a pile. She tipped her face back as the netting slapped her in its fall.

Holding on to the branch with one hand, he moved her to his side with the other arm until he could kick the end of the hanging hammock off the chair. Then he set her down again, leaped to the grass and reached up to swing her down in front of him.

"What is it about us," he asked, "that you don't see working?"

She looked wide-eyed and startled, as though surprised to be finally free of her net. "We've had this argument over and—"

"Well, let's have it one more time," he insisted. "What is it?"

"You're not only autocratic," she accused. "You're possessive! Even Natalie noticed it."

That surprised him. "I thought Natalie and I got on well."

"You did." She angled her chin. "She thought it was a good thing. I don't. A woman wants to be allowed to be who she is. No one wants to be... owned."

So that was it. He'd never quite understood the problem before. And as he saw it now, it was probably worse than he'd thought.

He caught her upper arms and, exerting great control, gave her just a small shake. "That, *necia,* is because she seems to understand that a man who is possessive about his woman..." He shook her again. "Are you paying attention?"

She was frowning at him and her lip was quivering. "What is *necia?*"

"It means 'silly,'" he explained tightly. "*Stupida* also came to mind, for which you wouldn't have needed a translation, but I chose to be the gentleman."

She firmed her lips to stop the trembling. "Go on, then."

"Natalie knew," he said, "that a possessive man doesn't want to own a woman's body or her soul—he wants her love."

He dropped his hands from her, suddenly worn out with loving her.

"But I'm thinking your love has too many conditions and sub-clauses," he said, climbing back up onto the chair to free the rest of the hammock. "You give very carefully, and I'm not sure I like that."

"That's because you have a history of taking what you want," she retorted.

She'd intended it to hurt, and it did. He'd been taken in to the criminal world as a child, but he'd chosen to stay as an adult—until he'd had to decide to make everyone stop during the Julie incident. He could live with what he'd done, but he hated that to be part of his child's background.

"You're right, *querida*," he said, reattaching the hammock to its base. "Maybe that's why you hold your love so tightly. I'm not the one you want to give it to." His task completed, he turned to her, a carefully controlled expression hiding the pain in his gut. "I came out here to tell you that Diego called and there's a problem with one of our clients. I have to go back."

"I see." The sound of her voice was liquid, as though it had emerged through tears.

"I'll simplify things for you," he said. "I'll file for the divorce. I'll assume the blame. And I'll see that you and Max are comfortable."

COMFORTABLE. Without him?

Dori watched Sal walk back into the house and experienced a sudden two-part epiphany.

First, she understood his point about being possessive. He'd wanted to own her love and he'd committed every kindness in the book to get it. She'd just been confused by vocabulary.

Second, it just occurred to her that the only way a woman could hold her own against a man who was just too much of one, was to be even more of a woman.

And she'd learned through her study of women of the past that strong women weren't always ladies.

Dori pushed her way into the kitchen and stormed

through a crowd of sisters-in-law who were peeling, mixing and cooking.

Julie caught her eye. "So?" she asked.

"So, I'm sorry I've left Max to you all this time," she replied, looking around the kitchen for him. All the children had left the table, and Max's high chair had been wiped off and placed in a corner. "Where is he, anyway?"

"Sal took him," Skye replied. "Mom and Dad are hosting a cartoon marathon with the rest of the kids."

"Good." Dori pushed up her sleeves. "Excuse me a few more minutes."

"Go," Julie said.

"Don't panic if you hear shouting," Dori warned.

Harper rolled her eyes. "We live with McKeons. Our ears are set at a higher register."

"Where are they, anyway?"

"They went to pick up the cake."

"All of them?"

Julie smiled. "I think they feared someone's retribution."

"Smart guys."

Dori hugged each of her sisters-in-law in turn and headed for the closed bedroom door.

Her mother looked up from the living room sofa and waved at her. Dori blew her a kiss. Her mother looked surprised.

Epiphanies all over the place, Dori thought.

She didn't bother to knock; Sal was her husband, after all. She had to clarify that.

She closed the bedroom door behind her and leaned against it, her knees weakened by the sight of Sal filling a suitcase. Max was sitting up, surrounded by pillows propped against the headboard. Cheddar lay curled up a safe distance away.

"Okay," she said. "That was rude and rotten and I'm sorry. I've never thought of you as a thief. Even the police didn't, because, when restitution was made, they let you all go."

He gave her a look that was weirdly disconnected, as though he'd somehow managed to cut himself off from her—from them.

"No need to apologize," he said, putting a stack of T-shirts into the bag. "I've often thought I wouldn't want a child to have that in his family."

When he turned his back to return to the dresser, she removed the stack of shirts. "That's ridiculous. To a child, that'd just give him status among his friends."

He had two handfuls of socks and, apparently prepared to stack them on top of the shirts, looked around as though he'd lost his mind. Then, seeing her replacing them in the dresser, he made a face.

"I'm not in a playful mood, Dori," he said, dropping the socks into the bag.

She ignored him. When he went to the closet, she removed the socks and put them back in the drawer. "What are you doing with Max?" she asked.

"Explaining to him why I won't be..." He stopped in front of the bag with several pairs of slacks and noticed the missing socks. "Are you campaigning to end up back in the hammock trap?" he asked threateningly.

She shook her head. "That was very uncomfortable, but very enlightening. It was like a metaphor for the trap in which I'd put myself. My whole life, I wondered how to fight my brothers, and then you came along—a man just like them—and you presented the same problem, only worse, because I loved you and wanted to bear your children.''

He looked puzzled. She liked that because he was always the one who had the answers.

''That must be why you kept us apart for two years,'' he said, his expression still uncertain but curiously removed, as though he wasn't sure he cared.

She had to do something about that.

''I kept us apart because I was selfish and...and *necia*,'' she said.

He dropped the slacks in the suitcase, then leaned back against the dresser and folded his arms, nodding at her use of his word. ''So you do sometimes listen to me.''

''I always listen to you,'' she corrected. ''I just don't always agree. And, *querido*, we're looking at a lifetime of my not always agreeing with you. But I won't let you overrule me every time. Because I've finally realized that the only way to hold my own with a man who's just too much of one is to be more of a woman than I've been so far.''

WELL, THAT HAD interesting possibilities, Sal thought. But he was still afraid to hope that this was going to work out, after all. So he simply listened. Behind her, the baby shouted and waved his arms, wanting someone's, anyone's, attention.

''No more whining and railing against you,'' she

said, going to pick Max up. "No more running away, pouting or otherwise behaving like a jerk. I will love you to the absolute best of my ability, but I will not lay down or roll over for you."

That was the point at which he lost his reserve. Laying down and rolling over were some of their best moves. "Ever?" he asked with a grin he was sure revealed every lascivious thought in his head.

She smiled, too, obviously chasing the same memories. "Well, maybe sometimes."

He drew a breath. Max reached for him, and Sal took the baby, thinking how much he loved the weight of him in his arms, his funny face now full of recognition and budding intelligence.

But he had a position to state here, too. "I understand and appreciate your declaration," he said, looking her in the eye. "I even applaud it. But please don't expect me to be any less your protector and defender because you've decided you're invincible. I've been around longer and in more dangerous places. I know you're not. You may consider yourself free as a bird, but in matters of personal safety, you will accede to my advice." That point made, he smiled again. "And I will lay down and roll over any time you ask."

She threw her arms around him and the baby, laughter deep in her throat.

"Did I mention that I love you?" she asked, looking up into his face, while the baby pulled at her ear.

Sal worked to extricate it from the grasping little fingers. "You did say something about wanting to bear my children. I think Max should have some company."

"Absolutely. A brother and a sister, at least."

"I like that."

Something seemed to occur to her suddenly, and she took a step away, looking unhappy. "Your trip..." she began.

He shook his head. "Was a fabrication. Diego didn't call me. I just didn't think I could stand to be in this den of deliriously happy McKeons if we were over."

"Oh, my darling," she said, holding him tightly again. "We are finally beginning."

She kissed him with what felt like complete conviction.

He kissed her with the promise that she was right.

Cheddar, as though understanding that all was resolved, moved to sit in the suitcase.

"What'll you do about the business? Do we have to go back to Seattle? I mean, I will, I just... wondered."

He'd given that some thought. "No. We'll look into the house behind the theater. I'll move our business headquarters here and Diego can manage the Seattle office. With computer hook-up and faxes it should be easy."

She hugged him fiercely again. "Oh, I'd love that," she whispered. She finally drew away and sighed. "We'd better go lend a hand out there. I've done nothing to help all day."

"Okay." Reluctantly, he backed toward the door and turned the knob.

As the door opened, Peg and all her daughters-in-law stumbled into the room. The brothers and Charlie, at the back of the small crowd, smiled innocently.

"Did I mention," Dori asked Sal dryly, "that there's no privacy in this family?"

Peg took Max from them and pulled Sal down to kiss his cheek. "But there's more love than you'll ever find anywhere."

* * * *

Don't forget Muriel Jensen's next WHO'S THE DADDY? *story*—Daddy To Be Determined— *is available in August 2002.*

SILHOUETTE SPECIAL EDITION

AVAILABLE FROM 19TH JULY 2002

THE NOT-SO-SECRET BABY Diana Whitney
That's My Baby!
Before mum-to-be Susan Mitchell told Jarod Bodine about their baby she had to find out what sort of father he was—by tutoring his son. But Susan hadn't expected to fall in love with the recalcitrant boy...or his father!

BACHELOR COP FINALLY CAUGHT? Gina Wilkins
Hot Off the Press
Police Chief Dan Meadows had always thought of Lindsey Gray as a sister. So he couldn't understand why, all of a sudden, he was noticing her curves. He couldn't be falling for her...could he?

WHEN I DREAM OF YOU Laurie Paige
Windraven Legacy
For generations scandalous secrets had divided the rival families of Megan Windom and Kyle Herriot. So how could one dance sweep them into a treacherous whirlpool of primal forbidden desire?

DADDY TO BE DETERMINED Muriel Jensen
Who's the Daddy?
Independent woman Natalie Browning had given up on love—but *not* on motherhood. Then she met single father Ben Griffin, who was honourable, intelligent, and *incredibly sexy*...her perfect daddy candidate!

FROM THIS DAY FORWARD Christie Ridgway
Annie Smith had yet to fall in love and everywhere she turned she came face-to-face with sexy Griffin Chase. But how could the housekeeper's daughter get involved with the heir to the Chase fortune?

HOME AT LAST Laurie Campbell
Detective JD Ryder was the only man that could help Kirsten find her three missing children. But she'd shared a past with JD and still kept a very special secret!

AVAILABLE FROM 19TH JULY 2002

SILHOUETTE®

Sensation™

Passionate, dramatic, thrilling romances

HARD TO HANDLE Kylie Brant
A HERO IN HER EYES Marie Ferrarella
TAYLOR'S TEMPTATION Suzanne Brockmann
BORN OF PASSION Carla Cassidy
COPS AND...LOVERS? Linda Castillo
DANGEROUS ATTRACTION Susan Vaughan

Intrigue™

Danger, deception and suspense

THE MAN FROM TEXAS Rebecca York
THE HIDDEN YEARS Susan Kearney
SPECIAL ASSIGNMENT: BABY Debra Webb
COLORADO'S FINEST Sheryl Lynn

Superromance™

Enjoy the drama, explore the emotions, experience the relationship

THE WRONG BROTHER Bonnie K Winn
THE COMMANDER Kay David
BIRTHRIGHT Judith Arnold
THE FAMILY WAY Rebecca Winters

Desire™

Two intense, sensual love stories in one volume

THE MILLIONAIRE'S FIRST LOVE
THE MILLIONAIRE COMES HOME Mary Lynn Baxter
THE BARONS OF TEXAS: KIT Fayrene Preston

SEDUCED BY THE SHEIKH
SLEEPING WITH THE SULTAN Alexandra Sellers
HIDE-AND-SHEIKH Gail Dayton

HER PERSONAL PROTECTOR
ROCKY AND THE SENATOR'S DAUGHTER Dixie Browning
NIGHT WIND'S WOMAN Sheri WhiteFeather

MARIE FERRARELLA
BEVERLY BARTON
LINDSAY McKENNA
DANGEROUS TO LOVE
3 SENSATIONAL, SEXY ROMANCES!
On sale 21st June 2002
0702/81/SH32

SILHOUETTE SPECIAL EDITION

is proud to present the all-new, exciting trilogy from

GINA WILKINS

HOT OFF THE PRESS

This small town's reporters are about to be shaken...by love!

THE STRANGER IN ROOM 205
July 2002

BACHELOR COP FINALLY CAUGHT?
August 2002

DATELINE MATRIMONY
September 2002

2 FREE
books and a surprise gift!

We would like to take this opportunity to thank you for reading this Silhouette® book by offering you the chance to take TWO more specially selected titles from the Special Edition™ series absolutely FREE! We're also making this offer to introduce you to the benefits of the Reader Service™—

- ★ FREE home delivery
- ★ FREE gifts and competitions
- ★ FREE monthly Newsletter
- ★ Exclusive Reader Service discount
- ★ Books available before they're in the shops

Accepting these FREE books and gift places you under no obligation to buy, you may cancel at any time, even after receiving your free shipment. Simply complete your details below and return the entire page to the address below. *You don't even need a stamp!*

YES! Please send me 2 free Special Edition books and a surprise gift. I understand that unless you hear from me, I will receive 4 superb new titles every month for just £2.85 each, postage and packing free. I am under no obligation to purchase any books and may cancel my subscription at any time. The free books and gift will be mine to keep in any case.

E2ZEA

Ms/Mrs/Miss/Mr ....Initials.......................................
BLOCK CAPITALS PLEASE

Surname ....

Address ....

....

....Postcode...................................

Send this whole page to:
UK: FREEPOST CN81, Croydon, CR9 3WZ
EIRE: PO Box 4546, Kilcock, County Kildare (stamp required)

Offer valid in UK and Eire only and not available to current Reader Service subscribers to this series. We reserve the right to refuse an application and applicants must be aged 18 years or over. Only one application per household. Terms and prices subject to change without notice. Offer expires 31st October 2002. As a result of this application, you may receive offers from other carefully selected companies. If you would prefer not to share in this opportunity please write to The Data Manager at the address above.

Silhouette® is a registered trademark used under licence.
Special Edition™ is being used as a trademark.